I0451792

BEREFT

Written By:
Jennifer Foor

Copyright © 2015 Jennifer Foor
JMF Publishing INC.
All Rights Reserved
Cover Art – **WICKED** *by* **DESIGN**

Thank you for taking the time to read Bereft, the second book in the seven year itch series. It is a stand-alone. It does include cheating, and is another story based on true events. I hope you enjoy it.

This book is a written act of fiction. Any places, characters, or similarities are purely coincidence. If certain places or characters are referenced it is for entertainment purposes only. Any resemblance to actual events, locales, organizations or persons, living or dead, is entirely coincidental.

No part of this book may be used or reproduced in any manner whatsoever without written permission except in the case of brief quotations embodied in critical articles and reviews. This book is not allowed to be offered for sale, discounted, or free on any sites not authorized by the author. This book may only be distributed by Jennifer Foor, the owner and Author of this series.

Sharing this book is illegal, and doing so will grant you the guilt of forever being a douchebag to society. Don't be THAT person everyone hates. Purchase a copy and feel good about your choices.

This book is dedicated to my wonderful husband. While I was writing this story, he suffered a massive heart attack leaving him with a life-threatening condition. I've always believed we could make it through anything.

The emotions written in this book reflect some of what it felt like for me to see him suffering. It has been hell. I thank God every single day for saving him.

We will get through this. Have faith and know you'll always have me, your biggest supporter.

I love you with all of my heart, Timothy Foor.

Beta Readers: Kristy, Kayla, Emma, Amanda, Teresa, Catherine, David – Thank you tons.

Dani: Without you this book would have been postponed. Thanks for pushing me and keeping me straight. Also, thank you Inkslinger for the love and support for my family. I will forever be grateful.

Chapter 1

The mirror doesn't lie. What I'm seeing really are wrinkles. I have crow's feet in the corner of my eyes, and when I'm not smiling I swear it appears as if I'm giving someone a resting-bitch face. What happened to my perfectly smooth complexion? Since when did I actually start looking my age? I hated being in my thirties – hated it. Since when did they stop carding me when I went to buy a bottle of wine?

This device my daughter had given me for Christmas made me want to reconsider walking outside at all. Who wants to see every single pore on their skin magnified to one-hundred? I wondered if she was secretly sitting at her dorm laughing, because she knew I was discovering things about myself that were terrifying.

At least I still had long, dark brown flowing hair, good health, and a handsome husband who continued to put up with me. It made it easier to appreciate my youth was now a thing of the past, even though I didn't consider myself to be old, just halfway there.

Usually mornings were easy for me. I'd get up, brew some fresh coffee for my husband, Grayson and I, and then proceed to get ready for work. From there, I'd drive to the train station, take the ride to D.C., walk six blocks to the office, and finally change into my fashionable pumps. The hustle and bustle of my job had paid off for my family. With my husband and I both working, we were able to pay for our daughter, well his daughter and my step-child, to attend a reputable college. We'd been empty nesters for over a year, and though lonely at times, Grayson and I enjoyed having our weekends to do what we wanted, because during the week we were both too busy, like passing ships in the night.

For nearly thirty years my husband had worked for an international shipping company, the one with the big brown trucks. He'd gone from delivery to upper management. While his positions changed, so did the hours. Where he'd been a six a.m. to three p.m. employee, had now changed to four twelve hour shifts. Each day he'd go in at nine, and he wouldn't get home until nine that evening, or a little after. I suppose he liked it, though it took me a while to get used to.

Lately, I hadn't seen much of him. When he was coming in the door, I was already in bed. Conversations were non-existent. While I normally rushed to get ready in the mornings, he was preoccupied with the sport's network. He would try to wake me up for sex, but I wasn't interested. Women need beauty rest – me especially.

I should have been happy about being younger than him, like I'd always be the trophy wife to my handsome silver fox. I felt like that's how he saw me, and us as a couple. We'd met years ago, back when he was going through a divorce. His ex-wife had been crazy – and I mean that in the nicest way possible. She was insane – clinically diagnosed with multiple personality disorder as well as being bi-polar. She'd been in an institution for years before committing suicide. It was a hard adjustment after it happened, testing not only my relationship with Stephanie, but also my commitment to her father.

They mourned, each in their own ways. I watched them fall apart, and did my best to bring them back from their lowest of times. I'd taken over as mother and caregiver for their daughter, without ever considering Grayson's opinion. She needed a female in her life, and even though I never overstepped, I wanted her to know she had someone there for her.

For me it was different. I bonded with the child immediately, even before the death of her mother. As far as I was concerned, she was my flesh and blood. I'd lay down my life for that girl in a heartbeat if I had to. She'd brought me so much joy in my life when I didn't even know I was looking for it.

Stephanie was a grown woman now. She was making her own adult decisions, as well as attending college and living on campus. Grayson and I were very proud of our girl.

Once we were married, things got easier. We had routines, and I suppose they worked for us. When you get to our age, mid-thirties for me, late forties for him, you're too set in your ways to want to change. You do what works to make life easier. So we stuck to our schedules, and spent time together when we could.

I smiled at my reflection in the mirror. Just thinking back to a time when we had struggled was hard for me. I liked to think I was the love of Grayson's life. He'd put me on a pedestal from the moment we met, and I'd never regretted a single second of our life together.

I took the tweezers and plucked a stag hair on my upper lip. I wondered how long it had been there, and if someone had noticed but been too embarrassed to say something. This mirror was making my morning dreadful, and also causing me to question if my husband was keeping things from me – like the stray hairs or large pores.

I suppose I'd been in an all-around bitter mood recently. I hadn't been sleeping well at night, which was giving me dark circles under my eyes. My doctor said it was stress, and to try to use relaxation techniques. He had no idea what I'd been worried about, and how nothing could keep it from happening. I had tried Yoga, and even meditation, which ended in me laughing at myself so terribly I couldn't continue.

Thankfully, Grayson never complained about my moods. It wasn't like they were taking away from our magnificent sex life, or lack there of. If we screwed around once a month it was considered frequent. It wasn't because I'd lost interest in my husband. He was gorgeous, and somehow getting sexier with age. I envied the way his skin stayed firm, and how he was constantly on the go.

When I got home at night, I wanted to kick back in pajama pants and relax while he got into projects, like painting, or jogging on the treadmill. He never seemed tired, like an energizer bunny with unlimited batteries. I read in bed until I fell asleep, most of the time having a Kindle hit me in the face when my lids closed before I could tuck it away.

Anyway, back to the reason for me being bitter. I'd received an email regarding a possible downsize. Employees weren't supposed to know about the owner's health taking a turn for the worst. The eighty year old man had battled cancer twice, and if you asked me, his body was tired of the struggle.

With that being said, everyone knew his grandson, Chad would eventually take over the company. His plans for a new future involved a ton of outsourcing. In fact, there were rumors he wanted to do away with the office and work off a remote server with minimal need for most of the people who worked there.

This would be the day where many of my co-workers discovered they'd lost their positions. I wasn't too concerned about mine. I'd been there since I was nineteen, and gained a good standing with the family. There was no way they'd kick me to the curb without prior notification. Aside from my husband, the owner was someone who cared for me. It wasn't in a romantic way. I'd like to think he considered me a daughter. His Christmas gifts were always lavish, and I'd been invited to attend family events for years.

His grandson, on the other hand, was a little prick. Sure, he had a body that wouldn't quit. It was obvious he spent most of his time at the gym, possibly beefing up with illegal injections of God only knows what. His eyes, a hazel in color, were constantly staring me down, and making me feel uncomfortable. He was like a dog on the prowl, and I was just a MILF, someone he fantasized fucking over his desk just to brag that it happened. Every week he'd storm into the office like he owned the place with a new bimbo attached to his hip. It made me want to gag, while his grandfather stated he was on his way to becoming a successful man, whatever that implied. Even though he'd attended college, I found him uneducated, or for a lack of better terms, worthless. If he was the last man on earth I still wouldn't stoop to his level, not even blindfolded, or blind in general. I was positive his brain was located at the tip of his penis, deprived of air, and suffocating in whoever he was nailing at the time.

Yeah, you could say I was resentful. Maybe a little.

Some of us have to work our asses off, while others are handed the silver cup. Life isn't fair, but us peons have to make it work.

Though the idea of being one of the only people left to work at his side, I knew I'd bite my tongue and make it productive. Besides, he'd need someone to show him the ropes when his grandfather could no longer manage. I wasn't hoping for a promotion; I was happy with my salary. I'd worked my way up in the company like everyone else. I didn't require special attention, especially when I knew it would cause my associates to question why they weren't being treated the same way. My boss Charles Farrow was a kind soul. He'd developed his company from the bottom up, investing most of his time into creating a reputable business.

Most people wouldn't understand how hard we worked for our clients, but in personal management, running an agency, nothing was considered too much. We went above and beyond, and carried a reputation to prove it. I was proud to tell people who I worked for and more to the point, which clients we represented.

Major corporations contacted us on a daily basis. I was there when we transitioned from landlines to mobile devices. I'd been an intern when the company went digital with their records. When PowerPoint became a thing, I was the person who taught upper management how to operate the software. My dedication had helped impact our future. We were able to keep up with the changing times, and offer the best degree of services because of it.

I was getting worked up over nothing, yet I couldn't stop pondering on my achievements, as if I was silently telling myself not to worry. It would have been nice to speak to Grayson about it, but I didn't want to alarm him for no reason. It was just another day at the office. Besides, I couldn't even recall the last time we'd had a serious conversation. It made me wonder what I could do to rectify the situation. I missed him – needed him even. He was my other half, my partner in life; it was important he knew what was going on with me. If anyone could calm me down, it was him.

My journey to the office only left me more concerned. I thought about the whispers I'd heard going on; the secret upper management meetings which lasted into the night. Then there were the conference calls where no one was invited except the owner's grandson.

Right before I was about to step off the train, I heard the alarms sounding. I was too familiar with what it meant. Someone had jumped onto the tracks to commit suicide, or possibly been murdered.

Talk about a Monday from Hell.

The doors remained shut and someone got on the intercom to make us aware of the situation. Luckily, I'd been early enough to score a seat, otherwise I'd be standing, waiting impatiently for emergency crews to arrive to cleanup and secure the area.

I blew a loose strand of hair out of my face, feeling annoyed I'd tied it up and it hadn't even lasted until I reached work. I thought about my pores, and how big they'd look after I had to haul ass a few blocks to make it to my morning meeting on time.

The longer I sat there waiting, the more I knew I was going to have to make a call into the office. I pulled out my cell phone and scrolled through my contacts, finally coming to the operator at the front desk. After a few seconds a cheerful voice filled the line. "Good morning, Leviathan Agency, how may I direct your call?"

"Sasha," I recognized the young blonde's voice. "It's me, Rachel. Someone jumped in front of the train this morning. I'm stuck here until they get it cleaned up."

"Oh no. I'll go in and tell Chad what's going on. I think everyone else is here already."

I sighed and thought about asking him to wait for me, but with twenty some odd people already in attendance, I couldn't do it. "Just tell them to start without me. I'll be there when I can."

"Will do. See ya soon."

I placed my phone back in my computer bag and looked around. I wasn't the only person annoyed. There simply was not enough time in the day to have a delay. What calmed me down was thinking about the poor family of the deceased victim. Had they jumped to their death? Were they pushed? Did they owe money? Were they in some kind of trouble with their health? So many factors could have been the reason for this type of incident.

I closed my eyes and thought about my step-daughter. Nearly twenty now, she had a full future ahead of her. She was majoring in Economics with a minor in Art. If it were up to her she'd live in a studio apartment, drawing pictures and selling them on EBay. She was simple. She didn't fret about the small stuff. Every day she found something to be thankful for. I took pride in raising her that way. She had a kind mannerism, and Grayson and I were often complimented for how she was taught to respect her peers.

I missed her being home, having someone to share meals with, even cuddle with on the couch while watching tear-jerking flicks. Just imagining going home to an empty house made me depressed. Most of my friends were going to be without an income after today. Facing them, saying goodbye, it would hurt my heart. I'd need emotional support.

Eventually we were released from the train and allowed to go about our day. They'd taped off the accident, and had an officer directing traffic to a different exit.

When I finally arrived at the office I was covered in sweat. I looked at my reflection in the glass window and tried to straighten up my hair, while switching my shoes to pumps. I think I made it into the elevator without taking a single breath, and pushed the button to my floor while gasping for air. When the doors opened, I was greeted by a smiling receptionist. "Good morning, Rachel. They're in the conference room waiting for you."

I rushed by her, hustling again to make up time. When I opened the double doors I expected to see a bunch of my coworkers sitting around the large teak stained table.

Instead, the owner and his grandson, Chad, were the only two remaining. "I'm so sorry I'm late. I ran into trouble on the train." I took a seat nearest to them and folded my hands together, ready to hear about everyone's reactions to the bad news." "It's actually good you're late today, Rachel. It gave us time to take care of some earlier matters." Charles replied. "Anything I need to know about?" My inquisitive question was meant to seem like I was oblivious to what had gone on. I knew they'd let a lot of people go already.

"I'm sure you were aware something was going down today. As you've probably guessed changes are being made with the company. My time here is about to expire, and we've," he pointed to the two of them, "made some decisions that will impact the future." His grandson, Chad, took over when he started to struggle with words. I knew he'd be bent out of shape over letting so many good people go. He wasn't the kind of man who liked hurting others, even if he couldn't help it. "What my grandfather is trying to say is we've decided to close the business, and start a new venture."

I folded my legs to prevent them from shaking, and prepared to be filled in on how we would be going forward for the rest of us left. "Okay. Will our positions change? Will the new company have some of their own employees?"

Charles, my boss for so many years, leaned forward and clapped his hands together as he struggled with an answer suitable for me to handle. I'd been around him for what seemed like forever, and never in that time had I seen him in such a state. The man looked as if he were about to cry. "Rachel, I'm sorry if you misunderstood. We're closing the doors on the company, for operational purposes. No positions will remain. I'm not in any condition to carry on, and my successor has declined to continue on the path we're on. He has other plans for our family legacy. It's best if we close with our good standing, and let a new firm step in. They'll take over the clientele, and offer the contractual obligations as severance. I know this is a shock."

I refused to let him keep talking as if this was a good idea. "Shock? You're sitting here telling me none of us have jobs, and all you can assume is that we're in shock? Charles, I've worked my ass off for those clients. I've taken time away from my family for some of those opportunities. I put my career before anything else, and you think it's okay to sit me down and let me go after all the years I devoted myself to your company?" I stood, because I simply wasn't able to sit there with his good-for-nothing grandson smiling back at me. I pointed to the man I'd always admired. "This isn't you. It's him. You're a good man. You'd never do this to the people you care about – to the clients who trusted their name with you."

I had to walk out, even though Chad had called my name for me to come back. Hot tears were pouring from my eyes. Nothing could save my job, so I, at least, needed to walk away with what little bit of reputation I still had.

Once I reached the main cubicle area, I was met with many emotional co-workers. Women were hugging and sniffling, while I could clearly hear some of the guys talking amongst themselves. Some were even on the phone, possibly with family or clients. They gave me disturbed looks and shook their heads. One guy, a techie, ambled over in front of my path. "Did you know? Did you know everything was going to shit?"

I cocked my neck and gave him a once over. "Did you? Don't you think I'd have the decency to make it to the meeting if I was aware what was going on? We're all in the same boat." I looked around the room and saw others had chimed in on our short conversation. "If I were you, I'd gather your things and leave the building. Take your client list and start making calls. If this is how we're going down, we're taking our people with us. Don't let that little prick take everything from us. We've built this company, all of us together. The people we represent will want to stay with us. We have relationships. Use them to your advantage. If the company is going to shit, let's leave it with nothing worth saving."

In unison several people agreed. For a second I felt empowered until I got to my desk and understood what had transpired. I was losing my job. Since I'd been in upper management, I didn't exactly have a huge client list. I'd passed that torch off to someone below me. I'd be shit out of luck, without a paddle in a very deep pool. They didn't say how long we were expected to continue, but from my standpoint I was done. Without regard for anyone else, I threw nearly twenty years worth of memories into a small paper box, including some office supplies they'd no longer be needing, and exited on the elevators.

Chad came running toward the closing doors. "Rachel, wait, please. We need to discuss this like adults."

I closed my eyes until I felt the machine operating. There would be no goodbyes, mostly because I couldn't handle them. I wouldn't want to. Looking in the eyes of the people who would struggle, lose homes, possibly everything, made me want to commit acts of murder on the little asshole upstairs. I hoped he choked on the large amount of money he'd be receiving for his grandfather's hard work. Guys like him made me ill. He'd probably invest it all in some gym that would be out of business within a year of opening its doors.

Because of my shock, I was unable to ask about my benefits, my retirement funds, and any kind of severance, not that it would matter. With a daughter still in college I'd have to struggle to find something else that would pay enough to get me by. I couldn't let this break me; or end her hopes of graduating from a four year university.

This was devastating – the end of living comfortably. At my age I'd be fighting people the same age as my daughter for a position. Companies weren't going to hire a washed up employee when they could pick up someone for half the money as a starting salary, and teach them the basics to get by.

This was a travesty. All I could think about was going home, putting on a pair of sweatpants and crying until my husband got home, which would be late in the evening. I thought about him holding me; somehow making my fears go away. Grayson was always good about that. He took care of us - of me. He would find a way to make things work. He'd take the stress off me, and convince me we were better off, somehow, someway.

For the first time since our daughter moved out of the house, I truly needed him. He was the only person in the world to make me feel better about this disaster.

Chapter 2

It wasn't until I made it to the train station when I really lost my shit. I sunk down on a vacant bench and bellowed out sadness. Several people stopped to ask if I needed assistance, but I waved them away from me without explanation. They couldn't help me, not even my husband could. He'd be as upset about this news as I was. For the time being, I had to keep it to myself, at least until I could break the news to him face to face.

My train ride home was a blur. I spent most of my time convincing myself I'd be okay. I mean, my husband made enough to pay our bills. We would make it work, no matter what we had to cut back on. So long as we had each other, nothing could break us.

When I arrived at home, I noticed my husband's vehicle parked the same way it'd been when I left earlier in the morning. He obviously hadn't left to head to the office yet. It was difficult to step out of my vehicle and know I was the bearer of bad news.

I walked slowly toward the front door, struggling to get my key inside the hole once there. Finally the door opened, and all was quiet. I didn't hear the normal sport's network blaring from the family room, nor did I hear him on his phone. Since I wanted to check my face before searching him out, I headed into the half bath and used the facilities.

At the same time, I heard voices coming from upstairs. I cracked the door because I swore I must have been mistaken, yet I was certain. My husband's voice was predominant. It couldn't be mistaken for another. The female voice was also familiar. I heard her giggling playfully while they carried on a conversation. Then it became quiet again.

Nothing, and I mean nothing, can describe how it feels to hear the sounds of your husband kissing another woman. As if my day hadn't been destructive already, I felt my whole life falling apart in that instant. Fear swept over me, and a million different scenarios played through my mind.

Was he having an affair?

Did I know her?

How long had it been going on?

Was I so naïve I didn't see a change in him?

What would happen next?

How would I survive?

How much would a divorce cost me?

Would I lose the support of my step-daughter if I left him?

Would she take his side?

Then there was the grief, and boy did it hurt.

How could he do this to me?

To us?

Why?

What had I done to deserve it?

When did our marriage start failing?

More playful banter could be heard echoing off the high ceilings in the foyer. I covered my mouth in disbelief. This was obviously a scandalous affair. The moans were louder, and I'd be an idiot not to recognize what my husband sounded like when he was getting off.

"Turn around."

"Right here on the steps? Mr. Grayson, you're a bad boy." More giggles and thumping. "Twice in one day?"

"I can't help it. You make me crazy."

The resonances allowed me to envision it playing out. Bile rose to my throat, imagining my husband balls deep inside of another woman, if she could even be called that. I recognized *that* voice. I knew exactly who *she* was.

This child had grown up spending half her time at our house, going on vacations with us, and celebrating holidays. I'd purchased her a Christmas gift since she was ten years old. *How could she come on to my husband? Had he come on to her? Was this a mutual attraction? How long had they been fucking around? Did she call him daddy? Did she want to?*

The more my mind wandered, the harder it was to remain silent.

I sank down to the floor and began to sob again, this time for a whole different reason. Never in my life had I felt so lost, used, and abandoned. Before I knew it the powder room door was being opened all the way. Grayson stood there staring at me, his face red, hair disheveled, and top unbuttoned. Behind him was my daughter's best friend, Kyla. I wanted to throw up when her eyes met mine, shocked and concerned. She couldn't begin to understand what she'd done, and how it would impact her friendship with our daughter.

I pointed to the door, gritting my teeth as the words came out. "How dare you? Kyla, I treated you like a daughter. He's like a father to you. This is over! Do you hear me? It's over! Get out of my house! You're no longer welcome here, and if I catch you anywhere near my family, I'll tell your parents what you've been doing."

"We care about each other. Grayson, tell her," she defended.

She was lucky I didn't turn around and grab the lid to the toilet, beating her with it until she was a puddle of nothing but blood. Normal human beings aren't capable of such violence. We know right from wrong, but in this instance, I totally could have done it without considering the consequences.

"Rachel, please," Grayson defended. "It's not what you think."

My finger moved in his direction. "Shut up! Just shut the hell up. Not what I think. Do I look stupid and blind? I want her out of here now!"

She was crying, not that I gave two shits. I watched

her run upstairs, then come back down with a handful of items. She didn't look back when she exited the home, I know because I watched her every step.

This was where I tell you I slit his throat and watched him bleed out. *Isn't that what every scorn woman imagines when she catches her husband with another woman?*

Okay, maybe that was a bit brazen. My first inkling was to hit him. I smacked my hands against his chest, pushing him backwards with each blow. My words made no sense as I screamed and cried to his discerning grimace. "How could you? How could you do this?"

He tried catching my violent arms to keep me from moving. "Would you stop and listen to me?"

Finally I did as he asked, but not because he wanted me to. I didn't have the strength. I couldn't begin to comprehend what was happening, and I didn't want to. My body was shutting down like it was going into a self-containment mode. I didn't want to feel anything, so I went blank, like a dormant machine being turned off at the source. "Get out," I whispered with barely the ability to say it.

"This is our home. I'm not going anywhere. I was curious, that's all. It won't happen again."

"Get out," I repeated, this time gritting my teeth. "She said you care about each other. This obviously wasn't the first time. I can't look at you. I'm sick to my stomach, and I want you to leave. You're not welcome here either."

"You've lost your mind if you think I'm going

anywhere, Rachel. I pay for this house. Maybe if you gave me attention I wouldn't have to go elsewhere. It's not like this should be a shock to you. We haven't been on the same page in years."

Truth be told, I was too comfortable. Life was monotonous. I never imagined he would stray. I never thought I had to keep one eye open because he'd do something so scandalous behind my back.

I'd never slapped my husband before, so when my hand came up and made contact with his stubbly cheek, I think for a second I felt guilty, until I realized how good it felt to express my rage. "How dare you? How dare you do something like this and blame me? This is your fault. It's your mess, and I suggest you start cleaning up. Now, I'm not asking you, I'm telling you, get out of this house. I can't look at you right now. I need to be alone."

He threw his hands in the air as he backed away and actually took my advice. He was probably going to run right to his little whore, where she'd mend his broken ego. Hell, he might get off on the fact that he'd been caught. Maybe this was how he figured he could get out of our marriage. Unlike a normal person, my husband was always a coward when it came to making adult decisions. Half the time he couldn't order take out on his own.

"See what I mean?" He argued. "It's always my fault. You don't make the effort. Its always me bending over backwards. At least I know you're still human now. You continue care a little about us. It's too bad you couldn't give a shit before, you know, all the nights you brought your damn computer to bed with you, and denied me affection. Did you think I could live like that forever?"

"You bastard! You could have come to me – talked to me like a committed husband should. You made the choice to sleep with someone else. You did this!" I could have killed him. His affair wasn't to get my attention. People didn't do that, not to the ones they love.

"I'll leave, but this isn't over. I won't let you take this away from me, Rachel. I've worked too hard for everything we have. We'll fix this. You'll get over it. I need you to. I'll end things with Kyla. It was never serious for me. I was flattered she found me attractive. One thing led to another and I couldn't help myself. You would have done the same thing had you been in my situation. Imagine being pushed away, feeling like you weren't attractive anymore. I made bad choices, because for once I wanted to feel alive again. You can hate me for it, but that's the truth. You're the only woman I'll ever love. I promised you that, and I mean it. You got me through the worst of times. I owe you everything. I won't let you push me away."

"You also promised to be faithful, asshole."

"You're right. I did. You made promises too, babe." Grayson seemed sincere while he was speaking, as if he truly was being honest about his feelings. "I'll give you a couple days to calm down. I'm not asking for you to understand, I'm not even asking for forgiveness. I made the choice to sleep with her. I know my sins." I looked into his eyes and saw he was beginning to tear up. "I'm sorry you had to find out like this. I never wanted you to know. In my mind I thought I could get it out of my system without causing strain on our relationship."

"I'm not ready to talk about this, Grayson. I can't." I shook my head and wiped my watered eyes. "I can't do this right now, not today. Please, I need to be alone."

Grayson marched up the stairs with his head down. I couldn't watch him gather his overnight bag and leave the property. Instead I went out into the sunroom and buried my face in a pillow. Some things were better left unsaid, at least until I could figure out what to do in response. I needed time, and possibly a divorce attorney. My gut feeling was to end my marriage, but I knew in time I'd miss him. After being married to someone I felt was my soulmate, I wasn't ready to throw it away for an affair. I was too strong to give up what I had, especially after losing so much. I could have given him more attention. I could have been more understanding when it came to his needs. Instead I'd pushed him away, thinking he didn't mind. I wondered how many nights he wished he were away from me? It hurt now to think about. In some ways maybe I had pushed him right into her arms.

While bawling my eyes out, I focused on the good in my life – our daughter. She was a perfect example of the love our family represented. I wanted to go back to a time where we were all so happy and have a do-over, because I knew no matter how hard I tried I'd never get the image of him fucking Kyla out of my mind.

Chapter 3

GRAYSON

"You heard what I said, Kyla. It was a mistake. I never should have gotten involved with you. I've ruined my marriage and possibly the relationship I have with my daughter. I need you to understand this and move on." I felt like a father scorning his child for making a mistake. The idea of it made me sick inside. I'd watched this girl grow into a young woman, never once assuming she'd get involved with me. Sure, I found her attractive. I wasn't living in a cave. Lots of people were attractive. That didn't mean I wanted to sleep with them.

When Kyla first came onto me it was out of the blue. My daughter had been visiting and she'd spent the night with her. That next morning, when my daughter had to head back to school, Kyla slept in. My wife left for work shortly after and I didn't have to be in the office until a few hours later.

"I thought we cared about each other," she whined through the phone.

"I do care about you, but not like you want me to. You've been a part of our lives for a long time. You're a good girl, but you've made a bad choice. We both have. This has to stop. I love my wife, Kyla. That's never been a question for me. This was always a temporary situation."

I could hear her sobs on the opposite end of the phone. "I feel used."

"I'm sorry for that. I wish I could say I wasn't a selfish man. Clearly I am. I took advantage of your generosity and got comfortable. I made decisions without considering the repercussions. Now I've got to figure out how to make things right. It's best if you steer clear of our house. I can't see you anymore, and I certainly don't want you around Rachel. She's been hurt enough. That woman has bent over backwards to do things for you. We've taken you on vacation with us. She loved you. I'm not the only one who broke her heart today."

"What if I love you?"

"You can't love me. You're confusing lust and infatuation with the real thing. Trust me, we don't have love. We've got nothing in common. I'm as old as your father. My daughter is your best friend. It's a crush, and I wish I never let it play out."

She was now in hysterics. "Why does it hurt so much?"

"Because it does. We've hurt people, and now each other. You're scared of what comes next."

I knew she was going to argue with me, though it wouldn't do any good. Nothing could take the pain away from the image of my wife's face when she'd caught me. I'd never regretted anything so much before. Now it was going to take a ton of convincing to prove to her how sincere I was about working things out. This girl was just a fling. She meant nothing to me, not in a romantic way. I never told her I loved her. If she assumed I did, it was her own fault.

"Please, Grayson. Don't do this to me."

"Do what? I'm being honest here. You're just a confused girl, Kyla. I said I was sorry. I don't know what else you expect of me. Once my daughter finds out what we've done, she'll never forgive either of us. I've probably ruined my life for a few good times. I know you don't understand, but I've devoted my life to my family, and now I've screwed it all up. They may never forgive me. I could lose everything."

"You'd still have me," she added.

"I can't do this. I'm hanging up. If you're a smart girl you'll lose my number and try to forget the things we did."

"Please don't…" I couldn't listen to her pleas any longer. I felt sick to my stomach. I needed to get a room and think about what I was going to do next. My wife didn't want to see me, and who could blame her? I'd fucked up. I'd let a little ass ruin my marriage, and that's exactly what it was coming to. Rachel was a strong-willed woman. She was set in her ways and liked being in control of the situation. I admired her strength, and the way she was able to manage multiple problems at once. This though, this broke her. I saw it in her desperate eyes. She was broken – lost – destroyed, all because I couldn't keep my dick in my pants. I saw an opportunity to feel young again and I dove right in, knowing the consequences would bite me in the ass at some point. I made the decision out of greed. I wanted to feel empowered; like I was able to get someone young and attractive. For a little while I felt like the king of the world. I thought I'd get away with it. The more it happened, the harder it was to imagine getting caught.

I suppose having her over to my house was the worst decision. I'd rather my wife have found out another way, so she wouldn't have been able to see and hear it. I didn't know if I'd ever be able to look into her eyes without seeing betrayal and hate. I was lucky she didn't find some way to murder me. I'd certainly never experienced her this upset in our years together.

I thought about calling my daughter, but what could I say? I wasn't going to tell her what I'd done over the phone. This was someone she thought of as a sister. As her father, I knew she'd lose respect for me. The thought of losing my little girl over this made me want to drive off a bridge. How could I have been so blinded by lust? Better yet, how in the hell was I going to fix the mess I made?

It took me a while before I could get my shit together enough to walk into a hotel and seek out a room. Once I did, I went inside and closed the door, looking around at the décor. Rachel wouldn't approve of this place. She'd say the linens were out of date, as well as the furniture. She'd complain about the germs found on the carpet, and even the remote control. I didn't even want to think about what she'd say about the bathroom.

I couldn't worry about what she'd think. I had to get myself together, and come to grips with the consequences of my actions.

After a long shower, where I actually wept, I wiped the steam away from the mirror and stared at my reflection. I hated the person looking back at me; the one who'd stray from his wife, his daughter, and the sanctity his family stood for. The person who'd put his own selfish needs before everyone else. I despised this man, and I didn't know how to overcome it.

I thought back to earlier in the morning when I'd

received the call from Kyla. She sent me a message of her in a towel. I dreaded looking at my phone and erasing it, because it would bring back the guilt once more. I'd been consumed by her. Everything she asked of me I did, like a little puppet. I wanted more, because what she offered blew my mind. I hadn't felt promiscuous since being a teen, perhaps I'd never been very adventurous in the sack, given the reason why I acted so reckless when it came to Kyla. Acting on impulse was easy, considering it had been a while since I'd been intimate with my wife. She didn't have to try hard to tempt me. That first time overwhelmed me. I couldn't help myself. I had to have her – to take what was forbidden. It was invigorating and terrified me at the same time. I'd never done something taboo, and the fact that it was with someone half my age – someone I'd known since childhood, well it made me feel like I was invincible.

The first time we messed around I didn't know how to react. We were sitting on the couch watching television. She was at the opposite end with her knees up to her chest. She kept fiddling with her fingernails, paying little attention to the football commentary happening on the television screen. I was engulfed in the show, following up on a game I'd fallen asleep watching. They were doing the highlights, running recaps of the top plays.

All of a sudden she stretched her legs out and touched the side of my thigh accidentally, so I thought. I gave myself a scoot in the opposite direction and went back to watching the show.

Then I discovered she'd done it on purpose. Her voice was calm, so collected, as she spoke. "Rachel is lucky to have a guy like you."

I didn't look her way when I responded. "Oh yeah? Why is that?"

"Isn't it obvious? You're so attractive for your age. Look at my dad. He looks old, like a grandfather even. You stay in shape. It's obvious you work out. I bet you have a lot of women hitting on you at work."

Her assumption made me laugh. In my twenty-nine some odd years working for the shipping company I'd had several advances, but they were quickly rejected on account of my values, especially while I was in my marriage. Still, when I smiled thinking back to them, Kyla noticed. "See, I knew it. Have you been a bad boy, Grayson?"

For the longest time I'd been Mr. Grayson. Since college started, Kyla had shortened it, like turning eighteen had granted her permission to refer to me as an equal adult. "What? No! This conversation is inappropriate don't you think?"

She adjusted the way she was sitting, sort of coming at me while still on her butt. "I don't know. I've seen you looking at me. I think you're experienced when it comes to getting your way?"

I turned off the television and sat the remote down, determined to head to work before it became any more awkward. "I better get going."

"What's the hurry?" Her question made me turn to look at her, because at that moment I wondered if she was losing it.

I should have never given her my attention. When I did, I watched as she lowered her tight blue tank top off her shoulder. "What's wrong, Grayson? Do I scare you? Haven't you ever fantasized about being with me?"

"No!" I was adamant. "Stop this. You need to get going, Kyla."

She crawled across the couch, breaking the distance between us. Before I could react by stepping backwards, she captured both of my arms. "I can't stop thinking about being with you. Don't you want to touch me?" I was ready to pull away, and then she sweetened the deal. "I won't tell anyone. It's just between us."

It was weird kissing another woman other than Rachel, at first. Kyla moved her tongue at a different rhythm and it took me a few seconds to match her groove. With every thought of stopping, I had more about going further. Suddenly my rational thinking went out the door. She pulled away and removed her top, tugging me down on the couch with her. I hovered over her, still intent on making out, like I assumed someone her age would want. She wasn't interested in that though. She wanted what was beneath my trousers. While kissing me, she used her skilled hands to unfasten my belt, then I felt my button coming loose. She shoved her fist down until she was able to put her hand around my dick. While steadily gripped, she jerked it up and down. I groaned and tried to rationalize once more with what I was about to do.

I couldn't stop it now.

I couldn't stop her.

I didn't want to.

Our clothes came off quickly. We met back on the

couch, until I slid off to examine her soft, curvy body. She let me touch her, and I felt chills down to my feet. She was perfect, and she wanted me, the old man she'd been around as much as her own parents. This wasn't right, which made it feel so good.

When I entered her for the first time I got lost in it – in her. I forgot about my responsibilities, my commitments, and above all, who I was. Kyla and I fucked right there on my couch not once, but twice. I didn't need a break, not with someone so seductive. She let me flip her over and take her from behind. She let me fuck her in her ass, and she practically begged me for it. The little temptress knew what she was doing. She was skilled in the male anatomy and took advantage of her knowledge. We spent the whole damn day naked. I felt like a kid again, and I think she recognized it. She kept taunting me with different ideas, and giving me more reasons to keep coming back. She knew I couldn't resist her, and when it was time for her to leave she gave me the hottest blow-job I'd ever received. I was captivated by her essence, and until she walked out the door, I didn't feel the least bit sorry for what I'd done, because in lieu of my actions, I'd rediscovered a part of myself that had been dormant for too long. I suppose that's why I couldn't stop it from happening over and over again. After time it was just normal to hook up with Kyla and go about my day. We'd fuck wherever we could, even at my office.

When I woke up this morning I felt good about life. I was getting away with murder, per se. I was involved with two women, one emotionally, and one physically. All it took for it to end was to see my emotional relationship fall apart before my eyes. It was a wakeup call, and now I had to come to terms with how it would impact my future.

Chapter 4

Tissues. How could we be out of tissues? I specifically remember there being three full boxes when I arrived home yesterday. As I pulled the very last one out of the square package, I recalled the past twenty-four hours.

Feeling as if I had nothing, I ventured over to the stairwell and looked around at the pictures strategically hung on the wall. So many memories filled my mind, all good and happy times. I wanted to close my eyes and go back to them, because thinking about the present made me want to crawl in a hole and die. Since I'd lost my job, and discovered my husband's affair, I'd considered drowning myself in expired prescription pills while lying in the hot tub. I wanted to close my eyes and never have to see or hear something painful again. After shoving those thoughts to the farthest place in my mind, I considered buying tickets to another country and reinventing myself, leaving this one, and everything in it behind. But I couldn't do that. I had a daughter to care for – and I was her only mother, even if she didn't have my blood in her veins. She was my reason for existing now, and I could never fail her. Yes, she was an adult, but she'd always need a mother. I had to think rationally, without regard for what I couldn't change. It was important to keep the good parts of my life in focus, because without it I was afraid I'd lose myself in depression.

That next afternoon Grayson began calling my cell phone. The mere sight of his number flashing on the screen made me cringe. When I closed my eyes to look away I saw him touching her in my mind. The excruciating truth was too new to fathom it ever going away.

By three p.m. I felt like death. I hadn't checked the slew of messages I was sure he'd left me, nor had I contacted work about further instructions. For all I knew I was supposed to report as if nothing was going on. I'm almost certain they wanted to stretch out the help for as long as they were able. I didn't have the energy or determination to leave the house, especially to travel so far for what was only going to frustrate me more.

When someone rang my doorbell I considered pretending I wasn't home. I waited a few minutes in hopes whoever it was would leave. I almost jumped when the doorbell rang a second time, right when I was about to peek out a window to see who it was.

Standing on the stoop was someone I never expected to see in my neck of the woods. I opened the door paying no mind to the fact that I probably looked like death. Chad gave me a once over and smiled. I went to close the door on his face, but he spoke quickly to change my mind. "Hold on, Rach. I come in peace. Please. My grandfather has been trying to reach you. From the look on your face, I can tell you've had a hell of a night."

"You don't know the half of it," I whispered under my breath while leaning against my door for support. "That still doesn't explain why you're here."

"I need your help, and since you packed up your things from the office, I figured you'd written us off."

I cackled in an annoyed manner. "You need my help? You're the last person on earth I'd want to help."

He motioned toward the foyer. "Are you going to invite me in?"

I cocked my eyebrow. "Why should I?" *Was I glutton for punishment? Did I really want more reasons to hate my life?*

He stuck his hands in his pockets and jingled some change around. I was surprised he was in a pair of jeans and a shirt with designs and skulls on it. The tight sleeves made his muscles look huge. It was rare, but I'd seen him dressed down before. He seemed more comfortable this way, instead of in business attire. "Hear me out. If you want me to leave afterwards, you never have to see me again."

The idea of that was intriguing. I tipped the door to imply he was welcome, even though I had immediate doubt. "The house is a wreck. I probably don't have anything to drink either, well not unless you want some bourbon."

"Actually," he walked inside and looked around. "That sounds perfect."

When he passed by I got a whiff of his cologne. He smelled magnificent. For a second I closed my eyes and took in the musk, pretending it wasn't coming from someone I despised.

I headed over to the liquor cabinet and located a newly purchased bottle. I'd picked it up for Grayson a week before, because I knew how much he liked to have a glass before bed. He wouldn't be needing it anymore, since he certainly wasn't going to be coming home to me. "Why are you here, Chad? I don't have the time or energy to deal with bullshit." I'd never talk to his grandfather that way, but Chad was another ballgame. I didn't care about disrespecting this little dickhead.

I spun around and noticed he'd sat down on the brown leather couch. He clapped his hands together and leaned back to get more comfortable. I don't know why, because he wasn't staying long. "You've got a nice place here, Rach."

"Stop calling me that," I requested, while handing him the glass.

"You look like shit. It wouldn't have been so bad for you if you'd just stuck around yesterday."

"You have no idea," I sarcastically added.

"After yesterday I wondered if you'd even want to be a part of the business."

"What business?"

"My new business. You see, Rach, I respect my grandfather, but he's an old man who can't see the future. I was born to be a leader, and that's why were closing the Leviathan Agency, per se. We're going into this with a new approach."

"I'm not following you, and again, stop calling me Rach."

"Aren't you sick of catering to a bunch of snobby

assholes?"

I rolled my eyes. "I'm used to being around assholes."

He let out a chuckle but continued. "Yeah, maybe you are. That's why I know this new venture will be right up your alley. How do you feel about commercials?"

"What?" I shook my head, not understanding this at all. "People hate commercials. Most fast forward through them."

The shit-eating grin was back. He nodded, but replied to my opinionated comment. "True. Some people do hate them, but what about the one person needing an extra push for his or her business?" He wiped the stubble on his chin and continued. "The clients we've been catering to for years need a firm they can trust. I'm talking commercials, music videos, video blogs, magazine articles, and billboards. I want to stop being the company who only gets a cut – a mere percentage of the profit."

"So, you want to sell off our clients to be able to open a video production company? Wait!" I thought to myself for a second and then it hit me. "You majored in what in college?"

"I double majored actually. Science and Marketing. That's a personal question, Rach. Do I get to ask you one in return?"

"No." I rubbed my hands on my yoga pants while trying not to feel uncomfortable. I didn't like Chad, and I certainly didn't want him in my living room, especially after discovering my husband was having an affair, probably on this very sofa we sat on.

"I'm going to ask anyway. Are you all right? Forgive me for being blunt, but I've never seen you look so…"

"Horrible," I answered for him. "I know. I'm sorry. Do we have to do this now?" I was starting to lose it. Of all people to show interest in my well being, he was the last I expected. It made me feel worse about my life.

"I'm here because I want you to be a part of the new company. It's going to take several months to get going, and of course we'll have to do everything by the books as far as legally utilizing our old clientele. I don't want to ruffle any feathers."

I sniffled, choking back tears. "You're offering me a job after you fired me?"

"We never said you were fired. If you would have hung around I could have at least briefed you on the idea. My grandfather is excited about this. He knows how much it means to me."

"What about his company? I know how hard he busted his ass to get where he is today?"

"We're selling off the shares slowly. The name will remain the same. We've got a buyer who is eager to purchase the majority of shares. It will go smoothly, and hopefully with your help, we can train the new staff to go above and beyond our average standards. In the meantime, we'll be managing both assets. I'm going to need a right hand person to help me. I'm asking you to consider it."

I thought about my predicament. My marriage was

in shambles, and I didn't know where my life was headed. Having a job to provide a roof over my head was a priority. "I'll help you until I can find something else."

When he smiled, one deep dimple filled his whole left cheek. "I'll take it." He stood up, finishing his bourbon before sitting it on the coffee table. "I'll be in touch about the details." He began to head toward the door. "You need to clean yourself up, Rach. You really do look like shit."

"Wait!" I called out to him. "What if I say yes?" I didn't want to seem desperate. "I'd like time to consider other options. When do you need my answer?"

"It's like a ghost town in there. Take a couple days. Think about my offer. It's going to be hard work, and a lot of long hours in the beginning. I don't want you to commit to something your husband might not be happy about. You need to do what's best for you. I just know there isn't anyone with your credentials who will give me the time of day at my age with a new company. You may think I'm a young, gold digging prick, but I'll prove you wrong. Being a businessman is in my blood. I'll make it work, or I'll die trying." He peeked his head in the door as he started to close it behind him. "You have my number. Call me when you have a firm decision."

When the door finally shut I stood there in shock. Yesterday I'd assumed the worst and left without hearing them out. The idea of working for Chad seemed horrible, but it would give me a sense of comfort I was going to need. No matter how sick I was over the company closing it's doors, I had the chance to stay employed.

I wasn't going to speak to Grayson about this opportunity. As far as I was concerned it was no longer his business. He lost his say in my life the first time he touched Kyla. For all I knew he'd been screwing around on me from day one.

As I turned around to head back into the living room, I caught my reflection in the mirror. Chad was right. I looked like death. No wonder my husband fell into the arms of another woman. I'd let myself go, and it was time to do something about it.

Chapter 5

Every five minutes I changed my mind about whether or not I wanted to work with Chad. He'd been such a cocky bastard for as long as I'd known him, yet his visit made me reevaluate what I thought I knew about the guy. I still had a feeling there was more than just selling the company, but something told me to stay out of it. I trusted Charles, but Chad was a different story. God only knew what he was truly up to, or if his new company would succeed or fail.

His visit did do one thing for me; it gave me something to look forward to. I hadn't committed, but for the sake of argument I would at least be bringing home an income if I needed to support myself. I spent the next several hours researching marketing firms. There were millions of companies out there offering the same services. Why would Chad think this was a good idea was beyond me? I mean, how could he assume closing a reputable company to open a new one was a wise business decision?

My all consuming mind wouldn't let me rest. By the time I realized I hadn't eaten anything, it was too late. I stood up and collapsed. The next time I opened my eyes I found myself on the floor. My chin was aching, but nothing else seemed to be injured. I wasn't bleeding, not that I could tell, and my teeth were all accounted for, thankfully. Just as I was standing up, I heard the front door opening. Alarmed, I turned my head around to see who it could be. My biggest fears were revealed when Grayson walked into my view. "Rachel? What are you doing on the floor?"

He took in the room, noticing two glasses on the table and a bottle of bourbon. "Are you drunk?"

I rolled my eyes and glanced in another direction. "I wish."

"We need to talk. I've been calling you all day." I knew he was staring at me, even though I couldn't peer in his direction to prove it.

"When I'm ready to speak to you, you'll know it. Until then, I have nothing to say."

He sat down anyway, ignoring my comment. "I haven't slept, and I've been sick since I last saw you. Please, babe. I know you're angry."

"Angry? Is that what you'd call it? You disgraced me. You ruined our lives."

"We can fix it. It meant nothing to me. I swear. You have to believe me."

"All I have to do is get away from you. Don't you understand? Can't you see how much you've destroyed our relationship. Nothing can erase the images I have in my mind –nothing. You've made your bed. Go lie in it with your little whore of a girlfriend."

His sobs didn't surprise me. I'd seen him emotional before, but this time I couldn't empathize. "Please forgive me," he begged.

"No. I won't." I started to cry. "I can't. I'll never be able to trust you again. Maybe it's best if we just call this what   it   is."
"What?" He asked.

"It's the end of us." My teeth were chattering as the words exited my mouth. It hurt worse than anything I'd ever experienced in my life. It was as if every single beautiful moment we'd shared had been removed from my mind. The only thing to remain was hate and betrayal. He'd killed my ability to see beyond his so–called mistake. Within the past twenty-four hours I'd lost too much. I couldn't consider patching things up, not now, and possibly not ever. "I need you to go," I managed to say.

"Tell me what to do," he continued. "Tell me what I have to do to make this right. I'm not giving up on us. You're everything to me. I'm so sorry, Rachel."

I covered my face with my hands, unable to control the emotions I was experiencing. As angry as I was with my husband, I couldn't bear to hear his pleading and not feel some kind of remorse. After all, he was the only man I loved, and even though he'd broken my heart, that kind of attachment didn't disappear. "I don't know. I can't answer that. I can't even look at you without feeling like my heart is being ripped from my chest. This isn't fair, Grayson. It's not fair to sit there and ask me what to do. You made this mess. I'm not the one who has to fix it."

My husband was bawling. He stood and walked into the kitchen to wash off his face. I managed to get up and make it into the bathroom, where I filled my hands with toilet paper and blew my nose. When it got quiet I headed back out and found him sitting on the couch with his hands folded. His eyes were bloodshot, and it was obvious he hadn't been to sleep. "Rachel, I love you. It's always been you."

I nodded, but didn't respond to his statement. Instead, I simply put on a brave face and sat down across from him. I placed both hands on my knees and held my head down to stare at the glasses on the table. "Like I told you before, I need time. I can't handle this. If you came here for forgiveness, you're not going to get it, at least not now."

"Tell me there's still a chance. I'll do anything. We can go to therapy. We can move to another location."

"Wait," I took a second to comprehend what he was willing to do. "You want me to uproot my life because of your mistakes? That's never going to happen."

He acknowledged my reply and stood to leave the room. I remained in the same position, stunned this was happening. A part of me believed it was all a terrible nightmare, and at any moment I'd wake and find him snoring next to me. I'd still have my job, and our happy life. I'd still have hope for a future with the two people who I loved with my whole heart.

I listened to him climbing the stairs. I heard the sounds of his dresser drawers opening and shutting. I even recognized the sound of a suitcase zipper. Then his feet were coming back down the steps, one by one, getting closer to leaving again.

A part of me wanted to beg him to stay. I wanted to take his ideas and run away where we could start over. I needed to be able to forget. I wanted to cross an ocean of sand, erasing the past with each mile we traveled. Then the rational part, whatever was left, knew it would never be possible. This would forever be etched into my brain, constantly reminding me of the pain, and broken promises. I had to be strong, for my dignity, for my sanity, but mostly for my future, if I wanted to have one.

"This isn't over, Rachel. I'll give you space, but I'm going to keep stopping by until you change your mind. We'll fix this, no matter how much time it takes."

"Goodbye, Grayson," I managed to get out before he closed the door behind him. It killed me inside knowing each and every time I pushed him away he could be running to be with her. I hated myself for thinking it. I wanted to believe he was sorry. More than anything I wanted him to hold me and make the pain subside. It just wasn't going to happen, because he was the cause of the pain. He was the reason I couldn't sleep, eat, or go into public without breaking down. I feared running into someone I knew who would ask about my family – about Grayson. We lived in a small area in the suburbs of Baltimore. Even though Maryland was a tiny state, it was overpopulated. Thankfully, we found a little historic town located near the train station, where I could ride into D.C. instead of having to commute by car. Amenities were an easy drive as well. The grocery store was less than a mile away, and there was a family-owned hardware store next to it. If we wanted to go big time shopping, or to a mall, we'd have to drive about thirty minutes. The people I didn't want to run into were the neighbors – every one of them. People were nosey. Most of mine were friendly to a fault. They knew everything about everything. I wondered how many had seen Kyla at my house and wondered if she was screwing around with my husband. I was curious to know if they'd been seen in public. The thought caused me to cringe. There was no way I could face the scrutiny I'd receive. I couldn't hear their whispers and not assume they were talking about me. I didn't want to.

"*Lord, please help me through this*," I kept repeating in my head.

I stepped over to the window and peeked outside, watching him get in his vehicle. For a few minutes he sat there with his hands covering his face. I could tell he was breaking down from the way his body was shaking. I put my hand over my face to try and contain the emotional pull it gave me. It was difficult seeing him in pain, and not being able to run to him. I had to be strong. I had to keep reminding myself that he was the enemy, for the moment at least. Until I could face him and not want to strangle the life from his body, it was best we were apart.

When he finally pulled out of the driveway I felt both relieved and alone.

Why was this happening to me?

I spent the night on the couch again, my eyes wide open, unable to close for fear of what I'd see when I fell asleep. This was the second night I'd gone without rest, and it was taking a toll on my sanity. When early morning came and I still couldn't relax, I guzzled the remainder of the bourbon, while holding my nose to elude the strong taste. I don't know how long it took it to do it's job, but eventually I found peace and passed out.

I didn't dream for the few hours my body rested. The morning sun awakened me, alongside of a killer headache. My cell phone had died sometime during the night. After taking some pain killers, I plugged it into the charger and decided two days was far too long to go without showering. The hot beads of water was almost as good as a deep tissue massage. I became more alert, and while I stood under the stream of the steaming waterfall. I started to see things in a different perspective. It was obvious I couldn't spend the rest of my life hiding out in a pair of overstretched yoga pants. I had to be strong, no matter what the outcome. I had to find resolution, because the ball was in my corner.

For the time being, I needed to focus on something other than my marriage. I was going to take the job with Chad, and hopefully it would keep me occupied, and help time heal my wounds. If not, at least I'd have money to feed my new bourbon habit.

Chapter 6

"Chad, it's me, Rachel."

"Caller I.D. has been out for a while. I know exactly who it is."

I hated his sarcasm. "I'm calling to accept your offer. I'll assist you with whatever you need to start the new company, but I have certain requests which need to be met before it's a final decision."

"Is that so?" he paused for a second, and I half expected him to have hung up. "I'll have a car pick you at four. Can you be ready by then?"

"Ready for what?"

"We'll discuss your terms over dinner. I've got a couple meetings this morning, but I'll be free and starving by this afternoon. That should give you enough time to jot down whatever you're thinking so we can discuss it."

I considered telling him I wasn't going to be seen in public with him, but this was about a job. It was appropriate and professional. "I'll be ready."

"See you later. Oh, and Rach..." I hated when he

called me that. "Please make sure you shower. Your hair was looking a bit sticky yesterday. I'll see you soon."

The call ended abruptly, and I could almost see the snarky look on his face after getting in the last bit of sarcasm before hanging up. The guy made me want to pull out my so-called *sticky* hair and scream. *Why did he think his shit didn't stink?*

It was weird how I hadn't been able to walk upstairs in my house in fear of finding the sheets in disarray. I'd showered in the downstairs bathroom to avoid it. I didn't want the image of Kyla and Grayson rumbling in my sheets to be a permanent photograph held captive in my over-imaginative brain. I creaked open my bedroom door and coasted the room with my eyes. The bed was made, just how I'd left it. Wherever they'd been screwing, it hadn't been in our bed, at least not this time. Still, instead of heading into the bathroom to freshen up for the second time, I began stripping the bed. I needed to bleach away any remnants of the two of them. When I had everything in a pile on the floor, I stared at it, thinking back to how many wonderful memories we'd made making love ourselves. I recalled the way he'd touch me, kiss and caress my skin, like I was precious and the only person to ever hold his heart. Grayson was an amazing lover. Imagining him giving that kind of affection to someone else made my stomach churn.

I promised to love and cherish him forever, for better or worse. This was obviously the worst possible scenario. I'd think I'd rather find out he was a cross dressing transvestite who longed to have a sex change and a feminine name like Precious. *Okay, that was a bit drastic, but you get my point.*

I fell down onto the plush gray carpet and curled up in ball, breaking down once again at the mess my marriage was in. For someone who hated the idea of an affair, I felt the need to know every detail about his betrayal. It made no sense. Why would I want to put myself through such horror? What good would it do?

Finally, when I felt like my tears were dried up, I got myself up and headed into the master bathroom. The white Carrera marble was cold on my bare feet as I stepped across it to turn on the spigot. I don't know what made me do it, but I looked down at the drain, curious to find a strand of hair that wasn't my color. I closed my eyes immediately and turned away. *I had to stop this.* Even if there were remnants, I couldn't change the past. I had to get over this looming darkness and move forward. It was how I coped, and the way I'd be able to forgive. Until I was willing to let go, it would never happen.

Aside from everything going on in my life, I was nervous about meeting with Chad regarding a new job opportunity. After speaking to him, it was quite obvious there was a lot of work to do between the old company closing it's doors and the new one opening. For many years I'd been involved in keeping our clients happy. I didn't want to imagine how they would feel to find out they needed to look for someone else to represent them. I had an idea for something that could work to everyone's advantage, but without the funds backing me, I wasn't sure it would be feasible.

It was amazing how washing my hair seemed like a daunting task. Moving at all was damn near impossible. If I could have stayed in bed for a whole month I still didn't feel like it would be enough time for my body and mind to recover from the stress I was under.

I stayed in the shower until the water turned cool. When I stepped out I walked up to the steamed mirror and wiped it so I could see my reflection. My eyes seemed sunken in, and there was little color to my face. The past few days had taken a toll on me, and if I didn't start pushing myself forward I was afraid my hair would either begin turning gray, or worse – thinning.

I hated the person staring back at me. For being much younger than my husband, he looked the same age. I needed a do-over. I needed to go back to the moment I began letting myself go and reevaluate what was important to me, instead of always trying to do everything at once.

Once I managed to dress in something other than yoga pants, I decided to go out and have my hair cut. It was time for a change, and what better reason to do it? My long hair was in need of a new appearance. Grayson had always preferred length. Since Kyla also had long locks, I longed to be different. If he couldn't appreciate the change, it was his loss. As far as I was concerned, I wanted to be the polar opposite of the girl who tried to steal my husband from me.

It wasn't long before my hair was full of foil in three different shades of dye. While waiting for it to set, I got a manicure, and instead of my usual French polish, I chose a dark red. It felt sexy and dirty; something I'd never been able to pull off before. I had my brows waxed for the first time in my life, and let me just say it wasn't a pleasant experience. A large welt was left where the hot goop was ripped from my skin. They said the swelling would go down eventually. *Lord I hoped so.*

Finally, my hair was rinsed and then cut. I think I

held my breath when I watched her take the scissors and cut at least ten inches off the back. My new style sat at my shoulders, and even with it still wet, my natural waves were coming to life. In the reflection I could see the three different colors as she smoothed my hair with a comb. The blonde streaks were a new addition alongside a tiny bit of red. Against the dark chocolate they really popped. Already it appeared that I'd shaved off several years from my appearance, making a small part of me feel good. Once it was styled, my hairdresser spun the chair around and let me see the finished product. I needed a good bit of makeup, but I still loved the new me even without it. I looked younger, sexy even. Then for a second I thought about Grayson, and what he would think when he saw it. I wanted him to be angry, like I'd done it to spite him, because in all honesty, I think I had.

My ride back to the house was much different than the morning. I wasn't dwelling in the negative. Sure, I still had a ton on my mind, but I was determined for one day to pretend my problems didn't exist. I had an opportunity to change my life, workwise, and it was important to remain focused so I'd be on my game when the time came to produce.

I'm not really sure why I thought it was a good idea, but I dug in my step-daughter's closet and pulled out a slinky black dress she'd worn to a New Year's Eve party. Since we were about the same size, I knew it would fit. Getting Chad to listen to me wouldn't be hard, but catching every bit of his attention would require a little scheming. I knew I'd feel uncomfortable in the dress, but I was going to pull it off. My livelihood depending on nailing this dinner meeting. Chad needed to know I was serious, and could do whatever was required in order to make it happen.

Since I didn't have to work on my hair, I focused on my makeup, going a bit heavier on the eyes than normal. I'd always been a light mascara kind of lady. Tonight I had on eyeliner and shadow. I'd looked online for a technique, attempted it three times, and finally figured it out.

I didn't know the person staring back at me, and I didn't want to. My real life was in shambles. It was a clusterfuck of madness. I was determined to be someone else for just one night. I needed to feel empowered, and this was the only way I saw it happening.

At three-forty five I heard a car pulling in the driveway. My heart started thumping as I took one last look in the foyer mirror. *"This was a mistake,"* I thought to myself. Before I could rush in the bathroom and wash off an hour's worth of makeup, the doorbell was ringing.

I tugged down the dress so it wasn't so high up on my thighs and took a few deep breaths, determined to act like nothing had changed. I assumed the driver would be picking me up, but instead opened the door to find Chad standing there. He was wearing a pair of dress pants and a button down shirt. His tie had been removed and the first two buttons near his collar were unfastened.

I loathed the way he took in my appearance, and rolled my eyes as he did it. "Excuse me, I'm looking for Rachel. Have you seen her? You must be her younger sister."

I shoved past him. "Shut up, Chad. I got my hair cut today, and my washer broke, so I had to wear something of my daughters."

He laughed from behind me. "You should dress like

this every day. Damn, woman, no offense, but your husband is a lucky man."

I froze. Not that I'd ever take anything Chad said serious, but his words this time were like someone putting their hands around my neck and slowly choking the life out of me. I didn't know how to respond, and I certainly didn't want this kid to know my personal business. "He is," I responded, before coming to realize we weren't going to dinner in the company vehicle. "What happened to the car?"

"Oh, my grandfather needed it for a charity event. You were supposed to attend, don't you remember?"

It had entirely slipped my mind. I felt like a disappointment as I stood there looking half my age in heels that were definitely going to break one or both of my ankles. "Shit. I forgot about it. It's been a hell of a week so far."

"No worries. If you'd like we could swing by after dinner. It's not a big deal. I'm sure he'd like to see you. My grandfather thinks highly of you. He warned me not to let you go. He told me it was important to do whatever necessary to keep you around and comfortable."

It wasn't how I saw things the other day, but I understood why he'd been hush hush. I'd never been able to keep secrets, especially when they involved people losing their jobs. "I have a heart. That's what he admires about me. Most people in our line of work look for the dollar signs. I've always enjoyed what we do."

He clenched his jaw like he was taking in what I'd said and processing it. It was strange how he wasn't looking at my body anymore, but more trying to read me from the inside out. I felt uncomfortable.

"We better get going. Traffic was a bitch getting here."

His steel toned Porsche sat low to the ground. He opened the door for me, while I struggled to find an easy way to climb in without my crotch displaying. I held onto the hem of my dress and basically fell into the seat, finally bringing my legs around in front of me. He closed the door without saying anything, and while he walked around to the driver's side I thought about getting out and calling it a night.

This didn't feel like a business meeting. I wasn't used to tight fitting dresses, or feeling sexy. I didn't have a dresser full of lingerie. I wore nightgowns and pinned my hair up. The person in this body wasn't me.

Why was I trying to change again? What had I done wrong?

I started to open the passenger door when he climbed in next to me. "What's wrong? Did you forget something?"

"I think I should change."

Chad reached over and touched my knee. I jerked it away as a gut reaction. "Don't. You look amazing. If you wanted my attention, you've got it."

I let the door close, but felt it necessary to explain. "I didn't wear this for you, Chad. Like I said before, I didn't have anything else to put on, and I wasn't sure where we were going. This is a business meeting, correct? I don't want you getting the wrong idea."

"We're on the same page. Forgive me for overstepping. Where are my manners? What I meant to say was that I like the change. You look happy. Good for you."

If he only knew how wrong he was. Inside I was the saddest soul. I just prayed I could get through the night without tears. I had to stay focused on my future, because without it I may as well have been dead.

Chapter 7

I'd been at the office but gotten nothing productive done. Kyla continued to call so many times I had to block her number. Then she somehow got the office number and tracked me down. I assumed I had a business call, but instead heard her voice on the other end of the line.

"This is Grayson."

"Why are you avoiding my calls? Did you block my number?"

I rubbed my temples as I spoke into the receiver. "Yes. I told you to leave me alone. Kyla, this has to stop. I need to repair my marriage."

"Why? You know I can make you happy."

"You don't know what I need. You never have. Sex isn't fulfillment. Please stop calling me."

"I need you. I feel like I can't live without you."

This girl was insane. She was going to stalk me, I just knew it. I closed my eyes and knew what had to happen. "If you don't stop this right now I'm going to have to tell Stephanie what's going on."

"You wouldn't. She'll hate you."

"At this point, I already hate myself. It can't get much worse than that. I'm asking you again, Kyla, please stop calling me. Whatever happened between us is over. It should have never happened. I hope you have a good life, but I'm going to need you to stay out of mine. If you know what's good for you, you'll cut ties with Steph too."

"She's my best friend."

"As far as I'm concerned, you betrayed her. She'll never forgive you."

"She'll never find out."

I hung up on her and asked my secretary to hold my calls. For the next hour I sat at my desk contemplating how I was going to tell my daughter what I'd done. She would hate me. She'd never forgive me. We'd been through hell when her mother passed away. The woman had been in and out of institutions her whole life. When she was on her meds she was a good person, but off them, she was a danger to herself and others around her. When she died it was like a weight was lifted. I no longer feared coming home and finding my child harmed or worse.

Rachel had come into our lives and picked up the pieces. She'd accepted Stephanie as her own and helped me raise her. We were married two years after first being together, and I never regretted a single moment of our marriage. Now I was determined to fight in order to save it, even if I had to throw myself under the bus to make it happen.

I waited until I knew she'd be out of her last class of the day to call. Dialing her number made the hair on my arms stand up. This wasn't how I wanted to go about ending my relationship with my daughter, and ultimately the bond she shared with her very best friend.

When she picked up the line, I realized there was no way I could break the news over the phone. We were going to have to meet.

"Hi, Daddy."

"Hey, babe. How's it going?"

"Good. What's up? Is everything okay?"

"Actually, I was thinking I could drive out and take you to dinner. Are you interested?"

"You'd drive an hour to take me to dinner?"

"I'd do anything for you. How about I pick you up around five?"

"Okay. Are you alright? You sound weird."

I knew I couldn't tell her the truth, because she'd be on the phone with her mother, and then she'd know the hard reality I was faced with. This had to come from me, not Rachel. We may have only been married for seven years, but she'd spent the past ten being the only mother my daughter had left. If something was happening between us she had a right to know. "I need to go so I can finish up. I can't wait to see you."

I hung up before she could press me for information. It was best to elude the truth until we were face to face.

I knew she'd hate me. There was no doubt in my

mind my news would break her precious heart. In order for me to make amends with Rachel, I'd have to get rid of Kyla. This was the right thing. Once Stephanie kicked her friend to the curb, I could focus on my marriage without having her stalking me.

I tried to call Rachel to let her know what I was doing, but as of late, she hadn't been returning my messages. It was difficult thinking about her being home alone, shedding tears, and facing unbearable pain because of my actions. I deserved the cold shoulder. Hell, I deserved it if she filed for divorce. I'd have no one to blame but myself.

I drove to the campus in silence. I didn't tune into the sport's channel, or listen to music. My head had to be mentally prepared for what was about to go down. It wasn't every day where I woke up and decided to break my child's heart. She'd been through enough. Had I thought about that before making such poor decisions, I probably wouldn't have been in this predicament.

When I arrived, I took notice of the young people making their way to and from the parking lot. They were just kids, yet I'd gotten involved with one. I felt sick to my stomach, not only because I'd done it, but because I enjoyed it. I was a pig. I didn't deserve my wife.

It took me a few minutes to settle down to where I was able to get out of the car without breaking down. This event was already taking a toll on me, and it hadn't even occurred yet.

Stephanie met me outside of her dorm. She was sitting on the steps peering down at her cell phone. I waited until I was right in front of her before speaking. She looked up with a huge smile on her face, stood and wrapped her arms around me. "It's so good to see you. Is Mom working late? I figured you'd be together."

She finally let go of my arms. I motioned for her to sit back down and took the spot on the steps next to her. "There's something I need to tell you."

"Is Mom okay? Oh my God did something happen to her?"

There was no easy way to start this. "Sweetie, your mom is okay. She's not speaking to me at the moment, but she's fine."

"Why? Did you two have a fight? I thought when the teenager moves out of the house the parents party it up. Were you sticking together for my benefit, because I know for a fact Mom loves you very much."

I appreciated her thoughts, but she could never be prepared for what I was about to say. "Your mother isn't talking to me because of something I did. I hurt her, and to be honest, I'm not sure she's going to forgive me."

I was already beginning to get choked up. I covered my face to keep the people passing by from noticing. My daughter put her hand on my shoulder. "Dad what did you do? Are you having financial problems? Is your job in danger?"

"No. I wish it were that simple." I took a few breaths and let it out. "I had an affair."

"What?" I could tell she was shocked. "When? Why? I thought you were happy."

"I am, I was. I got caught up in the excitement of it. I never planned it, and I certainly didn't mean for it to continue."

"So Mom knows?" She asked.

"Yes." I began to cry. "She caught me."

Steph tucked her arm inside mine and held it there. She leaned her head on my side. "Please don't cry, Daddy."

"I can't help it. I've ruined everything. Your mom didn't deserve this, and neither do you. I just thought it was best you found out from me."

I finally calmed down and stopped being such a baby. I deserved this fate. Rachel would want the bystanders to call me a pussy and take away my dignity. I'd certainly done enough damage to her to warrant it.

"Do you love the woman?"

She still didn't know who I'd been with. "No! Absolutely not. There were never feelings for me. It was just sex."

"How did Mom find out?"

"She caught me." I turned and looked out at an open field. The sun was beginning to set, and plenty of young adults were sitting around, reading and enjoying each other's company. "She came home and I was there."

Steph placed her hands up to her mouth. I could tell she was in shock. "I'm sorry, Steph. I knew better, but I went through with it anyway."

"Jesus, Dad." She didn't call me Daddy, which meant her opinion was changing. "How could you? No wonder she's pissed. Did she know the woman?"

"I'm afraid so."

She seemed intrigued, and I knew what she was going to ask next. "Do I?"

I took her hand and looked right at her, as if it would help the blow. "Honey, it's Kyla."

Steph jerked her hand away. She stood up and stared at me, like she could see right through me. "No. There's no way. Not my Kyla. She wouldn't. You wouldn't. That's sick!"

"Please hear me out."

She pointed to the parking lot. "You need to leave."

"I can't go. We have to talk about this. She came onto me. She said things to me, and threw herself at me. I'd never make a move on my own. I never even considered it."

"Please stop. I can't hear this. I feel like I'm going to be sick." She held her abdomen. "This can't be happening. I just talked to her. She wants to get together this weekend. She asked if she could stay the night. This is a bad joke, right? Tell me it is. It has to be."

"I'm afraid it's not a joke. The last time you were home Kyla stayed the night. You had to leave for a class the next morning. After your mother left for work she came down and sat on the couch with me. She started making comments about the way I looked. I ignored her, but then she began taking off her clothes. I don't know why I went through with it, but I did, and then it continued."

"This is disgusting. She's my age, Dad. How could you? She's like daughter to you."

"She was. I'd always thought of her that way, but things changed. Your mom and I haven't been on the same page and I appreciated the attention. It was selfish, and I hate myself, but that's the truth."

"I can't look at you. I'm so angry right now I could kill someone."

"Please don't. We need to handle this as a family."

"A family? Dad, do you hear yourself? We're not a family. Mom won't get over this. I wouldn't if I were her. Maybe it would be forgivable if it were with a stranger, but you screwed my best friend. An accident is once, but you've mentioned it went on for a while. That means both of you were sneaking behind our backs. Because of your actions our family might break apart, and I'm losing my best friend, because obviously she's lied and used me to get to you. How could I have not seen it? She's been mentioning you, asking me questions."

"Honey, I'm not going to give up on your mother. I can fix this. I promise I won't stop trying."

"I still want you to leave. I'm going to need to make a call and break up with my best friend. It's going to be ugly, and honestly, I don't even know if I'll be able to handle it. She's my oldest friend. I trusted her with my life."

"I hate to ask you this, but I need your help. I'll leave you alone. I promise I'll give you time."

"What do you want? I think you've taken enough from me, from mom." Stephanie wasn't letting up. She was pissed and hurt. I couldn't blame her. I never would. These were my sins.

"Kyla's causing problems. She won't stop calling me. I can't make good with your mother if she's still trying to contact me. I've asked her to stay away, but she refuses. She says she's in love with me."

She covered her face and shook her head. "Spare me the details. It's making me ill."

"We need to sever ties with the girl. She's starting to act crazy."

"You do realize you're asking me to give up my best friend? Do you have any idea how I feel about you right now?"

"I do." I glanced away. It hurt too much to see the disappointment in her eyes. I was no longer the father she looked up to. I was someone who'd made a mistake that could cost us our family. "Please help me make this right. I wouldn't ask if I wasn't desperate."

"I need to be away from you so I can think. I need to call Mom. It's going to take me a long time to be able to consider forgiving you. I can't imagine how Mom is feeling."

I reached over to kiss her, but she backed away. "You don't get to do that. You don't get to be my dad right now. You need to get out of here and make things right. If you've broken up our family I'll never forgive you."

I nodded and turned to walk away. I was well aware

it would go down the way it had, but nothing could have prepared me for the tornado of emotions I'd experience. My actions had cost me everything. I'd have to start from the bottom. I didn't care how hard it would be. I'd get my wife back, and I'd prove to her I could be the man she depended on to love her forever. I had to. I didn't think I could live without my girls, I wouldn't want to.

Chapter 8

I should have known he'd have good taste in food. He drove us into Baltimore, stopping only for the valet to be able to park his vehicle. He came around to my side and helped me out of the car, making me feel like it was more of a date than business meeting. Chad winked when he caught me giving him a inquisitive look. "Don't worry. I'm just trying to be a gentlemen. I won't bite."

I wanted to giggle. If he thought I'd let him touch me in that way he had another thing coming. Chad didn't know I was having marriage problems. As of a few days ago, neither did I. Of all the places I shouldn't have been, it was here, right now with Chad. Grayson expected me to be home, sobbing my life away. Instead, I was about to have a beautiful meal, and discuss the possibility of a new project.

With nothing else going right in my life, I had to keep my game face on. I let him lead us through the restaurant to our seats. He pulled out the chair for me, waiting for me to sit before taking his own. "Thanks. You can be yourself, Chad. I've been around you enough. I remember when you were just a kid running around the office."

He spread his napkin on his lap before ordering a bottle of wine from the waiter. I smiled and followed his lead, lifting the menu up to read. "Do you come here often?" I asked.

"It's my favorite actually. My mom used to bring me here when I was little, before she got sick."

Chad had lost both parents before the age of thirteen. His mother, Charles' oldest daughter, died of Leukemia. His father had been killed when Chad was only five in a severe accident. I remembered hearing Charles talking about it once. Foul play had been involved, but the case was closed shortly after, and the police never explain why. When the boy's mother got sick, they moved in with her parents. After she died, Charles and his wife gained custody. He'd been with them ever since.

I knew it was better to change the subject. "What should I order?"

"What do you like?"

"To tell you the truth, I'm so hungry I could eat just about anything. It's been a rough couple of days."

He snickered and watched as the waiter brought a bottle of red to the our table and began to pour it. "I bet." He sipped at his drink. "I should have asked if you ate meat. I couldn't remember."

"I eat meat. I don't have diet restrictions. I'm a mom, remember?"

I tasted the wine, letting it swish around on my palate before swallowing. "Yeah, what's that like, raising a step-child? Was it hard at first?"

This was an easy answer. "It was a tough transition

at first. Stephanie's biological mother was clinically insane. After she committed suicide, it was easier to gain her trust. I think in a lot of ways, she needed me to get through her loss. We've been close ever since."

"You never wanted kids of your own?" His questions were quite personal. We'd never been friendly in the office. In my opinion, I'd say he knew I disliked him, yet having a conversation about anything other than my husband's infidelity was acceptable. "I can't have children. It's a long story I'm sure you're not interested in."

"I'm sorry to hear that." He downed his first glass of wine. "I suck at small talk."

"It's okay," I replied. "It's kind of weird being here together, for a business meeting of course. I mean," I had to correct my statement. "I'm not used to dinners about work."

He smiled again and traced the edges of his wine while the waiter came over and refilled both our glasses. "Are you nervous being here with me?"

"No. Of course not." It was obvious I answered way too fast. He smiled before addressing the waiter with his order. I decided to have the same, and thanked the gentlemen as he took our menus and walked away. "I'm not uncomfortable. If we're going to be working together we need to discuss things."

"I get the feeling you can't stand me."

"You did barge into my house yesterday. I've never been paid a personal visit."

"I'm not talking about yesterday, Rachel. You've never liked me. Be honest. It's okay. I'll just have to work harder to convince you I'm not a monster."

"I never said you were."

"Ladies love me, Rachel. It's not a secret. I'm sure you seen them fawning over me. It's probably for the money, but I'd like to think I have more than my family fortune to offer."

This was the cocky Chad I knew and loathed. "I think it's best if we get to business. I have some ideas I want to run by you."

I sat there drinking my wine and explaining how I wanted to keep the agency open for our clients. I offered to run the whole division, where he wouldn't have to get his hands into it at all. I even explained how I didn't have the money to buy him out, but I would work my ass off to make sure it was profitable. Money was money. If he had me running the old company, he could focus on his new project. If he failed, he'd have something to fall back on. His family name would remain intact. He had nothing to lose.

"My grandfather suggested the same thing, but said it would be too much for you to take on."

"Trust me, it's not. I can devote one-hundred percent of my time to this job if you give me the chance. It's a win-win."

He sat there for a moment thinking to himself. "You want to devote all of your time to this? Have you spoken with your husband? I'm sure he doesn't want you working that far away at all hours of the night. Granted, it won't be every night, but still, problems happen."

"What my husband wants isn't my problem." I finished my second glass of wine. Just hearing him being addressed made me want to run out of the restaurant, take a cab home, and drown my sorrows in whatever alcohol I could find. "He's not staying with me at the moment."

"Since when? I saw you together at the company picnic."

"Since a few days ago," I answered. "Since the day I found out the company was shutting it's doors."

Chad adjusted the way he was sitting. "Man, I'm sorry. That explains why you were so upset the other day. You should have said something."

I watched the waiter come over and immediately fill my glass. I wanted to tell him to stop, but I needed the alcohol, especially now when my life's drama was out on the table for the little prick to pick at. I took a few fast sips before continuing. "I couldn't say anything. It hadn't sunk in yet."

"Did you kick him out?" He immediately threw up his hands. "I'm sorry. It's none of my business, and it's certainly not why I asked you to have dinner. I'm bad at that. My mother used to call me Nosey Nelly. That or Tattle Tail. You could say I was a little shit stirrer."

I smiled, appreciating him being comfortable talking about his own childhood experiences, instead of prying into my life. To be honest, he was the only person I'd been able to talk to since this started happening. It wasn't like I could call one of mine and Grayson's mutual friends and tell them what we were going through. I wasn't sure I wanted anyone important to us to know. I hadn't even told our daughter. "I caught him with another woman in our house that day." My confession wasn't easy to get out, and it was just as difficult watching Chad react to it.

"What the hell? Are you serious? You actually caught him?"

I nodded. "Yep." It wasn't hard to finish off another glass of red. The more I drank, the less I felt.

"Tell me you didn't know her, Rach." He seemed genuinely concerned. "Say she wasn't a friend of yours."

"She's my daughter's best friend." My eyes began to sting. I knew I had to excuse myself to the restroom, because I was about to lose it in front of the whole restaurant. "Sorry. I'll be right back."

Once inside, I entered a stall and locked the door. Toilet paper wasn't as soft as my aloe treated tissues, but it did the job. My makeup was running down my cheeks, and all I wanted to do was go home. I'd ruined the business meeting. What Chad thought had been small talk had caused me to lose my shit. I couldn't face him. It was embarrassing that I'd blabbed to him in the first place. It only made me feel more desperate.

After a few minutes I came out and started washing my face. I never expected him to come looking for me. "You okay?"

"What are you doing in here?"

"I made you cry. I had to make sure you weren't

falling apart."

"Too late. I'm a mess."

He smiled and handed me a paper towel. "Do you want to get out of here?"

"I want to remain focused, so we're able to talk about the business, but I'm afraid it's just too soon. I can't keep it together. Every little reminder sparks the emotions. I'm a freaking mess."

Then Chad did something that shocked me. He pulled me into a hug and held me there. I didn't wrap my arms around him, but I also didn't back away. I needed this type of support. I needed to feel like I wasn't alone, even if we were standing in the ladies room of a reputable eatery. As inappropriate as it was, I couldn't move.

He held me for a few minutes, until a female came in to use the facilities. He looked me straight in the eyes and spoke. "I'm going to get our food boxed up. Wait here. I'll come get you when the car is out front."

I nodded and watched him leave me. It wasn't the time or place to act this way, but I couldn't help it. The wine was making it worse. I rarely drank, and one glass was my limit. I didn't think I was slurring words, but I also wasn't in any condition to handle myself in an appropriate manner.

Within five minutes he was back in the restroom, offering me his arm to escort us out of the establishment. We didn't speak until we were in the car.

"I never should have pried, Rachel. I'm sorry I got you upset."

"You didn't. It's not your fault my husband had an affair. It's not your fault I wasn't good enough for him."

Did I really say that out loud?

"I'm still sorry for bringing it up. Let's get you home. We can talk about work when things settle down."

"No. I need this job, Chad. You don't understand. My marriage might be over. I need to have my own income. Please, if you have any heart at all, you won't turn me away. I'm desperate. I'll do anything you need. Just say you'll think about it."

His jaw kept clenching, but he didn't respond. We took the beltway home, cutting the travel time in half. When we pulled up in my driveway I expected him to drop me off and pull away, but Chad didn't do that at all. He jumped out and helped me to my feet. Then he grabbed the food containers and followed behind me.

"Is it okay if I eat before I leave? I'm not a douche, but I can't eat pasta in my car while I'm driving."

"Sure, if you don't mind my sniffles, or the possibility of me going homicidal."

"Nah, you're good. I've been around enough women to know how it is."

Right, because he was manwhore. How could I forget? One day he'd be married and cheat on his wife, like Grayson had done to me.

I headed up to my room to change out of the ridiculous dress I thought I'd looked sexy in. Now I felt like a big fat mess. Chad would never respect me. He'd never see me as his equal or more. My chances of continuing the agency were probably next to none, yet I couldn't tell him to leave. The truth was, I didn't want to be alone. I'd rather share a meal with someone I'd thought of as the enemy than sit alone in my home – the home my husband had fucked another woman in.

That's how pathetic I was.

Chapter 9

I'd definitely had too much to drink. Weighing in at a buck twenty, my small figure couldn't handle alcohol. I never could. Like the bourbon had done the day before, I was starting to feel exhausted.

I knew I couldn't pass out on my bed with company still downstairs, so I quickly tried to lift the dress over my head in order to change and get back to him. Unfortunately, the fastener got stuck in my hair. I yanked, willing to pull out strands to rectify the situation. The more I tugged, the more increasingly tangled it became.

This was just my luck. I managed to make it into the bathroom blindly. I fished around for the vanity drawer and felt for the pair of scissors. Once I had them in my hand, I tried my best to cut my way free. The dress was so tangled up, it was almost to my scalp. Never in my entire life had something like this occurred.

I took a chunk out of the dress, discovering afterwards I was still attached to another part of it. *For the love of God! This is horrible.*

When I tried to lower the dress back on, it only seemed to pull more hair. I sank down on the marble floor and began to growl out profanities. What was I to do? Did I yell downstairs for Chad to finish and find his way out? Did I dare ask him, of all people, to come upstairs and help me? The idea of it made me hate myself.

A man's voice startled me. It was low and apologetic. "You okay in there?"

Chad was standing outside of my bedroom. He was being respectful while checking on my condition. He'd probably heard me losing my cool. "You're going to laugh if I tell you what I've done."

"I promise not to laugh. I heard you yelling. I'm not comfortable being in this part of your house, but if you were in trouble I'd never forgive myself."

"Oh for shit's sake," I whispered under my breath. "Just come in and help me. I've already made a fool out of myself. It can't get any worse than this."

It was good I couldn't see his reaction when he walked into the bathroom and found me in my predicament. I did hear a slight laugh before I felt his hands examining the problem. "How the hell did you do this?"

"If I knew, I'd be able to get out of it."

"Did you cut off a piece?"

He'd obviously seen it on the floor. "I was trying to get free without having a bald spot. Can you please just hurry up. I've never felt more embarrassed in my life. I promise I won't bother you ever again. You can forget about the business deal. I know when to give up, and if this isn't a sign then I don't know what is."

Finally, I felt the fabric loosening. Chad lifted the

rest off my head. The first thing I noticed was the way he was taking in my body. I quickly covered myself with my arms. "Turn around."

"Sorry. I couldn't help it. I'm a man, and you, well you have a great body, Rach. You've got nothing to be embarrassed about. When I said your husband was a fool, I meant it."

He was quiet for a second, so I turned to look in his direction. He licked his lips and gave me a once over again. "I'm not someone you can fawn over, Chad. Get out of my bathroom."

"Can't a guy get a thanks?"

"Thank you and goodbye. It's best if you leave now. I've had enough embarrassment for a lifetime." In all honesty, I wanted to fill up my bathtub, take a bottle of bourbon, and drink until I sank to the bottom and ran out of air. This was devastating.

I backed Chad out of my room, but he never turned away from looking at me. Before I shut the door in his face, he reached out and stroked the side of my face. "Thanks for the good time, Rach. I think we're going to make a great team."

I was appalled. I stood there speechless as he turned and walked down the stairs. While I scrambled to dress and lock the door once he'd gone, I was shocked by the doorbell ringing. I pulled on a pair of cotton shorts I ran in, and a tank top, just to be clothed enough to answer it.

When I walked downstairs I was aware it wasn't going to be Grayson or Stephanie. They both had a key. I wondered if my husband had sent me flowers, but then again it was getting late, and I was pretty sure the delivery company didn't work past a certain hour.

I found Chad standing in the foyer. He was smiling when he saw me, once again checking out my body inappropriately. I rolled my eyes and headed to the door, determined to kick him out, and reject whoever was on the other side.

I never would have expected to see her standing there, hands on her hips, like she owned the place. "We need to talk," Kyla addressed while barging in.

I slammed the door shut, forgetting I already had company. She gave him a curious look before continuing into the living room. "Where do you think you're going, Kyla. You're not welcome here."

"I don't give a shit what you say to me. You need to know I'm not giving up on him. I love him, and I know he loves me too. He's wanted me for years. When he came onto me I didn't stop him. I loved every moment of it. We fucked in every single room of this house. He's mine, Rachel. He doesn't want you anymore, so stop trying to convince him otherwise. He's moved on."

Was she serious? Had she come into my home to threaten me?

"You need to get out, before I make you leave." I wasn't about to cry in front of her. She didn't deserve the energy. "If you and Grayson want each other so be it. I'm not trying to get him back. I don't want anything to do with either of you. You both used me and lied. I'll never forgive you. Now, if you don't leave right now, I will be forced to remove you from my home with force. I can promise you, it won't be pretty. You see, I've got nothing left to lose, so I don't care if I have to spend time in prison. I'd sit in that cell with a smile on my face knowing what I did to get you to leave."

She huffed and puffed, and finally stood to exit. "Who are you?" She asked Chad? "Is he your pool boy? Have you moved on so soon? Wait until Grayson hears his precious wife is fucking around with someone else."

"Screw you, little bitch!" I said while clenching my fists. In all my life, I'd never harmed another human being. I was a lover, not a fighter, but this bitch had pushed me to my limit.

"Bitch, get the fuck out of my face. Who I am is none of your damn business. You heard the lady, get the hell out," Chad responded adamantly. His eyes were stricken with rage, and I couldn't remember ever seeing him so offended. Maybe the idea of being with someone like me was repulsive to him. I didn't even mind, because he was giving her hell, and I liked hearing it.

"Fuck you both! He's mine, bitch. Just remember that." Kyla announced as she slammed the door behind her.

In that moment of despair I simply lost it. I collapsed down on the floor and began to sob uncontrollably. I didn't give a shit who was still in my house. I didn't care if he thought I was an ugly hag and wanted to run far away from my madness. I just didn't care about anything.

Chad surprisingly made his way over to where I was. He lifted me up and carried me over to the couch. Once I was situated, he sat down beside me. The two glasses from our bourbon were still there. "Where's the liquor cabinet?" He asked.

I pointed without speaking, then watched him get up and retrieve a bottle of something. I didn't care if it was special to Grayson. As far as I was concerned, Grayson could choke on his own tears and die. He'd destroyed me. Everything about my life was a mess. I was tired of crying, being fragile, and feeling as if I had nothing left to lose. I was exhausted, ready to give up.

Chad handed me a glass. "Drink it."

"What is it?"

"It doesn't matter. You need it." He downed his own glass. "Jesus Christ this is fucked up. So that's her?"

"Yep. That's her."

Chad patted on my knee. "She's a piece of shit. You should have kicked her ass."

"I'm sure you would have liked the show."

"No. Actually, I wouldn't have let you go after her. She's not worth it. Chicks like that aren't worth the energy. If your husband thinks she's an improvement he needs a reality check. She's trash, Rach. She'll never be as good as you are. You have to know that. She disgraced herself. It's obvious she's insecure. He probably told her to get lost and this is her last attempt at destroying everything he cares about. I've dealt with broads like that bitch. I know it hurts, but you can't let her get to you. She's beneath you."

"Who are you and what have you done to the little prick I can't stand?" I don't know why I said it, especially after he'd been so kind to me.

He chuckled at my comment. "It's me. Sometimes what you see isn't what you get. I was raised to respect people. You're a brilliant, sophisticated woman. You deserve to be treated like one."

"Thank you," I said with trembling lips. He made me feel like I had a reason to hope. "You don't have to stick around. I know I've ruined your night. I'll be fine. I'll lock the doors and probably pass out."

He looked around the living room and into the open kitchen. "If it's okay with you, I think I'll stick around. If that bitch comes back you don't need to get involved. We'll call the police and let them handle it."

"I can't ask you to do that. I'm sure you have other places to be."

"We need to be friends, Rach. A prick would walk out on a woman when she's hurting. I'm trying to prove I'm not that guy."

"I have nothing to offer you, Chad. Nothing."

"I didn't ask you for anything."

"I'm sorry she assumed you were my lover." Just saying it made me embarrassed. He must have thought I was a crazy person. I was almost old enough to be his mother. There was at least twelve years between us in age.

"I've been called worse. I think it offended you more than me. You're a beautiful woman. Any man would be honored to be considered your lover. It's all good."

"You're being too nice. Maybe you could tone it down a bit. I'm starting to think you're full of shit."

"I tell it like it is. If you were mine, I wouldn't let you slip away. Beautiful girls are a dime a dozen, but you have brains and a heart. You're not after a pot of gold. You're real to a fault. I enjoy your company. It's different than I'm used to. I think we're going to get along just fine."

"Sure, now that you've seen me half-naked."

"Rachel, even if I saw you completely naked, my opinion wouldn't change. Hell, I probably shouldn't say this, and if you want to slap me it's cool, but if you're ever needing someone to help you get over him, or even a revenge fuck, I could be that guy. No strings. I'm not looking to get settled down right now. I don't have time for a relationship. I'm telling you because I want you to know you're worth it. Your husband made a huge mistake, I'm sure of it after seeing that crazy cat."

I almost laughed through my constant tears. "Thanks for the offer. I'm not interested in revenge. It would hurt me worse."

"Like I said before, I'm just putting it out there. Sex doesn't have to mean something. It feels good. It's for pleasure. You're going to slap me now, aren't you?" I shook my head. "No. I'm not. I'm flattered. But it's still a no."

"Yeah, I figured. Why don't you go upstairs and get some sleep. I'll be fine on the couch. When you get up I'll be gone. I've got an early morning appointment I can't miss."

"Are you sure you want to stay?"

"I'm cool. There's pillows and a blanket. That's all I need. Can I use your shower in the morning before I go? I've got a change of clothes in my car I keep."

"Sure. The towels are under the sink in the bathroom on this level." I stood and turned to walk upstairs. "Chad, thank you. It's been an awkward night. Even with your offers, I still feel safer because you're here."

"Don't mention it. My grandfather would kick my ass if I let shit happen to you on my watch. Try to get some rest. If you need anything just ask," he snickered. "That includes physical favors." He shook his head. "I'm sorry. Some parts of me can't hold back. Your new haircut is sexy as shit. Goodnight, Rachel."

"Goodnight, Chad."

Chapter 10

My drive home from the college was unbearable. My daughter hated me; that much I knew. She was adamant on me leaving, and I wasn't sure how long it would take her to forgive me for what I'd done.

It wasn't just my betrayal. She was screwed over by her very best friend. We'd shared a secret. It was the ultimate disloyalty.

Infidelity had led me down this path. Now I didn't know what to do to remedy the situation. Once again, I tried calling my wife. No answer.

I even attempted to contact my daughter. It went straight to voicemail. Both of my girls couldn't stand the sight of me.

When my phone rang I felt excited. I figured one of them was calling to say they wanted to talk. I didn't care what direction I needed to turn the car in. I'd run to them if I had to.

The number was unlisted, but I answered anyway. Rachel could have gotten her number changed, but decided to give it to me anyway. "Hello?"

"Hey, baby it's me. I took care of our little problem. You don't have to worry about Rachel getting in our way any more. I know she's the reason you don't want to see me."

"What are you talking about? What did you do? If you harmed her at all you'll be sorry."

"Calm down. I didn't touch a hair on her body. I paid her a visit, and told her to leave us alone. We're too connected to end things. We can be happy. She'll be out of the picture and you me and Steph can be a family. It will be like old times."

What the hell was happening?

"Kyla, listen to me. There is no us. What did you say to Rachel?"

"I told her to leave us alone. She knows we fucked all over your house. She knows there's not an inch of that house you didn't have me in. Face it, Grayson, I'm all you have left. Rachel doesn't want you. She told me I could have you. Now there's no reason for us to be apart."

"You're insane. Do you hear yourself? Even if Rachel hates me, I still won't love you. I never have and I never will."

The line was quiet. "You'll change your mind. You'll miss me. I know you will. Give it a couple days. You'll be begging to see me."

"No. I won't. Stop calling me, Kyla. I'm having my number changed. This is ridiculous."

I was infuriated. She'd gone and screwed my life up worse. I didn't even think it was possible.

It was late, but I had to get to Rachel. She needed to

know I hadn't put Kyla up to the visit. She had to know she was a liar. Yes, we'd had sex in a lot of places, but there were things which needed to stay buried. Details would only hurt her more. I couldn't deal with the agony of imaging what Rachel was going through.

I drove fast, not even stopping when my gas light flickered on. My wife was hurting, and I was the only person who could help alleviate what she was feeling. I needed her to believe me. I needed her to still love me.

I never expected to pull up to the house and see a car in the driveway, a Porsche at that. The tags were registered to a D.C. address, so I figured it was someone she worked with. Maybe she'd asked a girlfriend to come stay with her while she went through hell. Maybe she needed the support of a friend.

I used my key to open the door. It was quiet and dark when I entered into the foyer. I sat my keys down on the small side table and went to turn on the light. When I did I got the shock of my life. A male, maybe a bit older than my daughter, was standing in front of me. "Who the hell are you?"

"I'm assuming you're the husband?"

"You're damn right I am."

"She doesn't want to see you."

"Look, I don't know who you are, but you need to tell me where my wife is." I glanced up the stairs and yelled for her. "Rachel!"

I could hear her walking around, so I turned my

attention back to the guy. He was shirtless, his hair disheveled on top his head. "Who are you?"

"A friend."

"Of who? Do you know Stephanie?"

"No. I'm a friend of Rachel. Now, I'm telling you, it's best if you leave. She's had a rough night."

"I know. I heard. That's why I'm here."

"Grayson?" I heard my wife ask. "What are you doing here?"

"I live here."

The look on her face said it all. "I want you to leave. As you can see I'm fine."

"You heard the lady," the young man added.

I wasn't taking shit from some young buck. "What are you doing in my house? Who are you? Are you fucking my wife now? Is that what this is? Are you paying me back?"

"You would think that," she uttered.

"I want to know."

"She asked you to leave, dude."

I shoved the kid back. "Stay out of it. I don't know who you are, but you need to be on your way. This is between me and my wife."

I turned back to Rachel, only to feel him shoving me this time. "What the…"

"Grayson, please. Don't do this. I asked him to stay."

"I don't give a shit." I pointed to the guy. "Get out now. I'm serious. One of us is leaving, and it isn't me."

"He's not going anywhere. I want him to stay. You're the one who needs to leave."

"It's been a few days. How could you replace me so soon? What's gotten into you? This isn't you talking. You wouldn't be so careless." Anger filled me. I didn't know what my wife was up to, but I wasn't going to allow her to push me away for another. If this was her revenge she knew exactly where to stab me. "Please. I just want to talk."

The guy took me by the arm, in my own house. I shook from his hold, turning around and swinging with all my might. "Don't touch me! Keep your hands off me."

Rachel rushed to his side, staring up at me with tear-filled eyes. "You need to go. I don't want to see you. You did this, not me. I'm just trying to cope the best way I know how. You have no right to tell me what to do anymore. You lost that when you slept with Kyla. She says you're not over, so go be with her, because I certainly don't want you anymore." Her words were like a sheet of glass, shattering all around me. She'd changed her appearance, her hair was shorter, and it was obvious she'd been wearing makeup. A man half my age was apparently sleeping over. Were they involved? Did she run right into his arms? How long had they known each other?

This was all my fault.

What had I done to my beautiful wife? Had I caused her to make unjustly decisions just to get me back? Was this guy even a friend of hers to begin with?

"Rachel, please. Don't say that."

Her friend was starting to stand up. She stayed at his side. I shook my head and back stepped toward the door. "This is what you want?" I pointed to him.

She nodded. "Just go. I can't stand to look at you. You've made your bed, now go lie in it. I told you before, I'm not able to forgive you."

"Well, I can't forgive you either."

"Screw you, Grayson. You ended our commitment to each other the moment you put your dick inside of another woman. You did this – all of it. Leave, before I say what I really want you to hear." She looked right into my eyes. "You know what, I don't even care how this feels for you. I.WANT.A.DIVORCE!"

It was the last blow. She'd crushed me. Whoever the guy was, she obviously preferred his company instead of mine. I'd been her everything, and now I was like the garbage she wanted out of the kitchen. Nothing could mend her heart. Her mind was made up. If it hadn't been before, Kyla had made sure of it.

I'd ruined my life for meaningless sex. Aside from probably going to Hell, I'd lost hope of mending my marriage. Maybe it was too soon to push. Maybe I should have stayed away.

Maybe I should have done a lot of things differently.

I had to face the facts. My marriage was over, and there was nothing I could do to change it now.

Chapter 11

I watched my husband walk out the door and said nothing. I didn't run after him and beg him to stop. I didn't regret telling him I was through. I was numb, momentarily. I wanted him to see what he'd done and regret it for the rest of his life. He needed to know he'd done this to us, and that his actions had put me in this position. Grayson assumed I was romantically involved with Chad, and I didn't correct him. It made me feel empowered over the situation. I had the upper hand, because instead of dwelling in sadness I'd picked up a hottie and brought him home to fuck mercifully until the name Grayson no longer existed.

"Are you okay?" Chad asked while standing beside me.

I turned and looked directly into his eyes. I knew it was wrong on so many levels, but I was brutally demolished when it came to my marriage. I needed reprieve, and I was desperate to do whatever that entailed. "Would you like to come upstairs with me?"

"You know it's a bad idea. Anger fucks are fun, but you'll be hurting worse in the morning."

"I'm afraid there is no worse. It's not possible. I've hit rock bottom."

"I'm not coming upstairs with you. It won't help. I can distract you, but the pain will still exist."

I'd never touched another man besides my husband since we first began dating. Seeing this half-naked specimen in front of me, one who'd done nothing but compliment me, protect me even. I wasn't worried about what would happen afterwards. I didn't care if it was awkward, because I didn't give a shit about anything anymore. My marriage was over. It was done. I wouldn't get past an affair of this magnitude.

"All I want to do is forget about everything for a little while. You can either come upstairs and help me out, or I'll do it my damn self. The choice is yours."

"Rach, you're mad. I get it. Once you cross that line, there's no going back. I can live with it, but I'm afraid you won't be able to. As much as I'd like to be the person to give a woman like you a good time, I need to say no. It's for all the wrong reasons."

"But you said…"

"I know what I said before," he interrupted. "It's different now. This shit is ridiculously complicated. I'm good with revenge, but I'm not okay with working next to you in the future and seeing the look in your eyes that I know you'll give me. It can't work."

It hurt. I'm not going to lie. Being rejected when I wanted nothing more than to relieve my frustrations. I knew Chad was right. Sleeping with him would be a mistake. The alcohol mixed with my emotions were causing me to make irrational decisions. I was angry, intolerable. I needed to justify my decisions before making them. "Fine." I spun around and stormed up the steps, realizing I was going to spend the night alone, in the bed Grayson had fucked his little girlfriend in.

I'd replaced the sheets, but after her little conversation, I couldn't begin to imagine myself sleeping on that mattress. I immediately began to cry, taking my pillows and putting them on the carpeted floor. I'd rather sleep there, then feel like their love making was overwhelming me.

I don't know how long I bawled. Time wasn't important. My life was in shambles. It was so pathetic I'd hit on my new boss; someone I'd hated for years. Now he was sleeping on my couch, worried about my well-being. I felt so confused.

I laid there staring at the ceiling fan for a while. I thought about Grayson, and the things he'd said to me when I discovered his affair. I thought about Kyla, and how she'd contradicted a lot of it. Then I thought about Chad. I'd been wrong about him. There was more to him than a nice body and cocky smile. I didn't know how I was going to face him after throwing myself out there. He must have been laughing the moment I walked away.

I was glad he'd stuck around though. Grayson was shocked to see another man in our home. The idea of hurting him made me happy. I wanted him to suffer. I needed it to feel like his heart was being ripped from his chest. It was important for him to know he was replaceable. In my heart I didn't feel that way, but I'd never lead on otherwise.

A light knocking caused me to sit up. I knew it was Chad, and I suddenly wondered what I was going to say. I stood up and made my way over to the door, cracking it open. It was dark in the hallway. I could barely see his face. "Yes? Did you need something?"

He cleared his throat, like he was giving himself a second to reconsider. "Can I come in?"

"What for?" I inquired.

"Look, you're older. You're married. It's obvious you're going through hell. Me being here is probably the worst idea, but I'm sitting downstairs and all I can think about is being close to you. I don't give a shit if you hate me tomorrow. It won't be the first one-night stand of my life. I can deal with it." He paused for a minute. "The thing is, tonight at dinner, you looked beautiful. That dress, my God your legs went on forever."

I pulled him into my room. "Shut up, Chad. Just shut up." His lips were on mine before I could blink. He was so tall he had to bend over. His arms easily went around my waist. He moved his tongue gradually, as if he was testing the waters. When my hands touched his bare chest his body felt hot and rock hard. His kisses seemed suggestive, allowing me to sample what else he might be good at. I felt his tongue enter my mouth and let my own glide against it. It was warm, inviting even. I couldn't stop myself. I wanted him closer, even though we were already touching.

Without warning, he picked me up in his arms, carrying me over to the bed. There was no time to tell him to go somewhere else. When I dropped down on the mattress, I was silently pleading for him to join me. I sat up, tugging on the button of his trousers. He stopped me and lifted my chin with one finger. "Are you sure you want this?"

I nodded, reaching for another kiss.

"What if your husband comes back?"

"Don't talk."

His lips brushed over mine leisurely. It was obvious he knew what he was doing. This person I'd considered a kid was proving me wrong. His touch was electric. Like a shock to my broken heart, he coursed his mouth over my neck, his tongue tracing lines as he went. I closed my eyes and felt nothing but pleasure. The pain ripping through me was dissipated. Though temporary, it was working. I wanted this. I needed to feel wanted. This man desired me. He was with me, and he was enjoying himself.

I didn't fight it when he lifted my tank top over my head. He held it up in the air, only visible by the light of the moon coming in through the large double window. When it dropped, I swear it moved in slow motion. His lips were on mine again, sucking on my bottom lip, pulling it until I wanted to cry out, then finally letting go. He drug his teeth down my neck, breathing deeply so it tickled. Both hands massaged my breasts. When I moved my hands to touch him, he took them and raised them above my head. I closed my eyes, feeling every inch of skin he was caressing.

My nipples were oversensitive. He licked over one, sucking the whole mound into his mouth. I could feel him circling his tongue over the tip, then biting it before letting go. He paused, blowing cool air over it. Using his thumb, he grazed it again, sending pins and needles throughout my body. My back arched as he repeated the process on the opposite side.

With my arms above my head, he traveled down lower, kissing my abdomen. He drove his tongue into my belly button, at the same time pinching my nipples. My pussy pulsated, like it was awaiting his attention. His strong hands worked their way down my hips. He latched his fingers over the elastic and tugged my shorts off my ankles, taking my panties with them.

I could feel I was naked without bringing my hands down to check. Chad reached over and turned on a light located on the nightstand. My hands came down over my breasts, feeling overexposed, and needing immediate coverage. "What's wrong?"

"Nothing. I need to see all of you. Sex in the dark is impersonal. I need to see your pussy as I eat it. I want to watch your face when I take you to the brink, and then witness you falling apart, and when we fuck, I'm going to watch my dick sliding inside your wet cunt."

I was panting. His words left me terrified. I'd never been so subjected, yet I wanted him to continue. I wanted to shove his face between my legs and beg him to get started. "What are you waiting for?"

He smiled while narrowing his gaze on his next pit stop. I inhaled and waited for his tongue to touch my bare skin. He ran his thumbs over a patch of hair over my pussy, massaging my clit as he worked his way down. He parted my lips, watching me watching him do it. That smile remained on his face. He sucked my pussy into his mouth, tugging while applying pressure with his tongue. I bucked, shocked my body would react so wildly. Chad's dark hair was all I was able to see when I looked down. He was lapping me up, taking his time with every inch of my tender area.

I still couldn't believe this was happening. Not only was I being pleasured, almost forced to forget my problems, but he was absolving my marriage. I'd decided it was over, but this made it final. There was no going back. The further I let Chad go, the more I knew I was headed for divorce. Seven years of marriage had been thrown down the tubes. All I could do now was look to the future.

My first orgasm was anything but anticlimactic. My toes curled. My body trembled, and I screamed out, so loud I was sure the neighbors across the street could hear. Chad lifted his head, while placing gentle kisses all over my spent pussy. "There's no turning back now, Rach." *Did he really think I'd stop him after that display?*

"I know." His lips came up to mine, and quickly he had me in his arms. His unfastened pants were lingering on his hips. I took my feet and shoved them down, leaving only a pair of boxers left between seeing what else he had been hiding from me. I could feel his stiff erection poking me as we kissed.

I was so horny – ready to pounce like a cat in heat. This younger man wanted to ravage me and I was prepared to let him. I could just lie back and take it all in, but I wanted to participate. When he was finished I wanted him to look back at our time together and say it was amazing.

Chad shoved his boxers down. We were too close for me to peek, but again, I could already feel that there was quite a bit of length involved. He bent down and took out his wallet, ripping a package and pulling out a rubber. "You come prepared."

"I like to be safe, Rach."

"I can appreciate that." It wouldn't have bothered me if he wasn't. I was at a point in my life where I wasn't sure I wanted to live another day in agony.

After he'd applied his protection, he picked me up and carried me over to the dresser. He sat my ass on the edge, pressing his hard cock between my legs. He rubbed it around, teasing my clit with the hot tip.

I was soaked – so much that I assumed he'd think it was weird. I couldn't ever remember being this turned on. I felt like I needed to grab a towel and wipe off already.

Chad groaned when he discovered my predicament. "How does it make you feel to know I did this you?"

"Good," I cooed.

"I want to fuck you so bad. My dick feels like it's going to explode." He lifted me, forcing me to stand in front of him. He led me over to the bed and bent me over the edge. "I need to see that ass." He began rubbing both cheeks. "Oh yeah. I knew it would be perfect the first time I saw you walk by me." He slapped my left cheek hard. I gasped, shocked he'd done it. When I said nothing he did it again, this time rubbing the underneath of my pussy. I felt fingers going inside of me, and then something touching my ass. I straightened my body, twisting around to face him. "Don't."

He cackled. "Don't what? Come on. Let me play."

I looked down, prepared to scorn him until I saw what he had waiting for me. My mouth dropped. I knew he had a perfect body, but I swore he'd lack a certain girth down below.

I was dead wrong.

He was hung like a fucking farm animal, and he knew it too. A half-smile formed in the corner of his lips. "What's wrong? Too big for that supple ass?"

"Too big for everything."

"Turn back around. I promise I won't hurt you. When I fuck you, you'll beg for more. I promise."

I don't know why I trusted him. My breathing was heavy. I could feel my heart having palpitations. I pressed my face against the mattress, with my ass remaining in the air.

He spread my legs, and then my pussy lips. I felt something cold hitting the hole in my ass, then a finger spreading it around. He'd spit there, and as he circled his finger around it, my pussy quivered. "Holy shit. Don't stop."

"What's that?"

"You heard me," I said with chattering teeth. I was nervous, yet prepared, scared, yet satisfied. It made no sense.

He penetrated my asshole, shoving his finger in as far as it would go. He kept at it, driving it deep then removing it. I could barely keep my knees from buckling.

Just when I was about to lose control, I felt pressure on my pussy. His thick shaft was making it's entrance. I sucked in a full breath as it slid inside me. He was so large it squeezed against my tight walls. I couldn't remember the last time I'd been intimate with Grayson, and I wondered if Chad could tell. He moaned and said things under his breath. I heard 'oh my God' several times. He thrust in and out until he was able to fit his whole cock inside of me. It was uncomfortable at first, the friction making it bearable. His finger started moving again, this time triple the speed. Being penetrated in both holes was a magnificent discovery. My body tightened up immediately and I exploded with another orgasm.

Chad didn't break for air. He spun me around and leaned forward to suck on one of my nipples. He bit the tip, so hard I was sure he drew blood. I screeched and sucked in a deep breath of air, only to realize the pain had quickly changed to pleasure. He pinched the opposite nipple, coming up to tease me with his tongue. I sucked it into my mouth, turning his taunting into a full-blown kiss.

Chad ran his hand through my hair, gripping a large chunk to hold my head longer. He was in control of our make out session, and I was completely okay with it.

With no hands, he teased my pussy with his dick. He gave it a shove and slid right inside. Immediately I was filled, and as he got into a groove I found myself jerking my hips to match his pace. He started doing it harder, slapping our bodies together. I wrapped my legs around his ass and moved opposite of him, making our contact more powerful. I was soaked, and each time we slapped together it made a noise. It was sticky, catching my clit and pulling it just enough to add to my euphoria. He held onto my thighs and really went to town. I could tell he was getting close. His face tensed, and his pattern was unhinged. Then I felt his fingernails digging into my ass cheeks. Once again I felt slicing pain, then a rush of rapture.

We were both shaking afterwards, maybe for two complete reasons. My marriage was over. I'd made sure of it. I'd slept with a co-worker; one I'd previously hated with a passion. Now the only passion he'd given me was in bed.

I didn't know whether to laugh or cry.

I ended up doing the latter, and Chad climbed up in the bed and held me until I was able to fall asleep. He said nothing – he didn't need to. He knew I was having regrets. He knew inside I was a mess, and that I would hate myself before I could learn to accept there were things in life I'd never be able to change.

Chapter 12

GRAYSON

That next morning I woke up still in the same clothes as the previous night. After Rachel kicked me out of the house, claiming our marriage was a thing of the past, I drove by several times, hoping to find the Porsche gone from the driveway. Instead, I saw the bedroom light on, and two shadows inside. It crushed me.

I finally understood what it felt like for Rachel. I was sick to my stomach imagining another man touching parts of her she'd promised would be mine forever. I'd been blinded, and awakened by the brutal truth of consequences – the kind you have to live with even though they break you.

The first thing I did once I got out of bed was attempt to contact my daughter. By now she'd had time to think about what I'd told her. I hoped she'd talk to me, but was disappointed when the call was sent to her voicemail.

"Baby, it's Daddy. I get that you're mad. Trust me, I hate myself for what I've done. The truth is, I need you. I've hit rock bottom, and you're all I have left. Please call me back. I'd really like to hear your voice, even if you're calling to tell me off again."

I hung up the phone and immediately dialed Rachel. I just wanted to hear her voice. Lucky for me, I got her voicemail too. "This is Rachel Lewis. Please leave your name and number and I'll get back to you as soon as possible."

I listened for the beep and hesitated. What did I say to her after last night. She'd pretty much sent me packing for a lifetime of misery. How was I to even approach her without some kind of caution? To make matters worse, I knew she'd screwed around with someone else to pay me back. It was immature, but I couldn't blame her. I knew what it was like to act on impulse. She was vulnerable, and at the right moment he'd be able to take advantage of it. He'd probably been hitting on her for months, just waiting for the right time to make his move.

I wasn't sure how old the guy was, but it was obvious he was still in his twenties. I'd been through a lot in my life, but never experienced this type of jealousy before. I couldn't compete – another reason which made it easier to relate to my distraught wife. She'd probably picked this guy on purpose, knowing if I ever found out it would be like a kick in the balls.

By nine-thirty I was on my way into work. I'd keep busy on work-orders, and try my best to make it through the day without leaving early. I had enough time accrued to take a few personal days, but didn't want to do it if I didn't have to.

Once inside, I locked my office door, taking a seat behind my desk. On it was a picture of my family, the three of us. We were all smiling, but what made the moment perfect was that Rachel and I were looking deeply into each other's eyes. The photographer hadn't told us to do it. It happened accidentally and she'd captured it. It was my favorite picture of us, and I'd had it on my desk since the very day we picked them up.

Back then things were easy. Rachel and I talked to each other. We came home every night and shared meals together. Our weekends were filled with adventures. Back then we were full-time parents. We had a mutual reason to work as a team. Things were different since Stephanie went off to college. The house was quiet, and my new hours had taken a toll on our relationship. I knew she was tired by the time I got home, but I'd felt like she was neglecting me. Why couldn't she wake up if I was in the mood? Was she tired of being with me? Did she stop missing me?

I suppose it was way too late to try to and fix what was broken. Still, my mind wouldn't let me stop wondering. I felt like if she'd give me a chance I could convince her to take me back, even though I think I knew it was a long shot. She'd made sure of it when she gave her body to another.

I tried to focus on my workload, first by checking my messages from the previous day.

The first one was from Kyla. "Hey, it's me. I'm just checking in. I know you said to leave you alone, but there's no reason we can't be friends. I miss you, Grayson. Call me back."

The next six messages were work calls, then two more followed from Kyla again. I hated she'd gotten the direct number to my office. To be honest, I hated her. If she hadn't come onto me, this would have never happened. I wouldn't have thought about her inappropriately, and I certainly wouldn't have made a move. I was a good man; a perfect husband, and I'd thrown it away so recklessly.

I considered calling some of our mutual friends to check on her, but I knew Rachel would get pissed off. She was always so damn adamant about other people knowing our business.

Since I was trying to get her to speak to me, I had to tread lightly. Rachel was like a ticking time bomb. I couldn't recall ever seeing her so verbally aggressive. This was a side of my wife I didn't like, and what was worse was that I'd brought it on. Now she was unhinged, acting on impulse and doing things she wouldn't normally be caught doing. She wanted me to suffer, and I felt it was necessary to let her know her plan was working.

I called her phone again, this time prepared to leave a message. When the chimed sounded I didn't hold back. "Rachel, it's me, Grayson. I'm hoping you won't erase this before you listen to the whole message. I love you. You need to know that first and foremost. You mean everything to me, and I know I fucked up. God, do I know it. I wish I could take it back. It wasn't worth it, none of it. Losing you makes me want to die. I already feel dead inside. I don't know what Kyla said to you, but she's lying. There are no feelings between us. She's crazy. I've never had any kind of emotional attachment to that girl. It was just sex." I paused for a moment. "I know what you did last night. I came back around and saw you through the window. If you did it for revenge I get it. I just don't want you to be hurt. If you need time I'll wait, but I'll never give up. Please call me. Let me know you're okay. I miss you. I miss coming home and seeing you sleeping. I miss the way you sneak around in the mornings to keep from waking me. I miss us, Rachel. I need you. Please don't give up on us. It doesn't have to be over."

After I hung up I wept silently at my desk. I never thought I'd be in this predicament. I didn't see my wife kicking me out, or losing her love. I'd always been so sure she'd be there for me for the rest of my life. Now I wondered if I'd have anyone. Maybe I'd live out my life alone. It was unbearable to consider.

Chapter 13

I woke up when the sun came in through the window. It was nearly seven in the morning. The sound of the shower was obvious, and for a second I thought it was Grayson getting ready for work. Then it all came rushing back.

I'd slept with Chad.

The Chad.

What was I thinking, right? What kind of women degrades herself the way I had?

I knew exactly why I'd gone through with it, and as every single second of our time together came back to me, I felt a smile forming across my face. Sure, there was guilt, but to what degree should I have felt bad for my actions when I was only trying to alleviate some of the looming pain I'd been under?

I didn't know what someone else in my position would have done. Maybe they'd be able to forgive their husband for his infidelities. Maybe I was just as terrible of a person for doing the same thing. However, in my opinion my actions were justified. With all the pain I'd endured, I felt I deserved to feel cared about, even if it were only a temporary fix. The image of Kyla and Grayson would forever be burned into my retinas. It may not have been right, but it sure as hell felt good either way.

I wasn't certain what to say to Chad. We'd obviously taken things too far, and I wondered if he was trying to rush out before things got too awkward. Maybe he was trying to leave so I wouldn't be able to talk to him about what happened. I stayed in bed, determined to pretend I was still sleeping when he exited the bathroom.

I heard him get out, and open the cabinets looking for a towel. I suppose I should have ran in and left him one on the counter, but I was too flustered to consider walking around with no clothes on, which was how we fell asleep.

Chad came out of the bathroom, steam still lifting off his wet skin. He was wrapped in only a towel from the waist down, not that I needed to be reminded of what was hiding underneath. I was probably going to be sore for a few days because of it.

I was surprised when he came over and climbed onto the bed, leaning over to brush the hair away from my face. "I need to get going."

"Okay."

"We should talk about that business plan soon. Let me know what day is good for you and we'll set something up."

"Okay." I realized I'd answered two questions in a row with the same response, but I was a little taken back.

"You have my number to get in touch with me,

right?"

"Yeah, I'm pretty sure if I don't it's easy to get." I sat up and tried to act professional. "Do you need me to come into the office today?"

"No. That won't be necessary. If I were you I'd take the rest of the week off. You're going through a lot of shit, Rach. Get things figured out first. I'm going to need a fresh head on you when you return."

"I can't promise a few days will fix everything that's wrong in my life."

"Yeah, wishful thinking," he said with a little chuckle. "Are we okay? I know last night was unexpected. I don't want things to be weird between us."

"I don't either, though I wouldn't blame you if you did feel that way."

"I'm good. Last night was intense. I hope you got something out of it."

"You could say that."

He raised his brow and seemed to be studying my face. "I better get out of here. I have an early appointment I can't miss."

He reached forward and kissed me on the cheek. *The cheek.* "I'll see you soon."

I don't know what I expected. I suppose I assumed he would go on and on about how last night was the best of his life, and he never expected to hit it off with me so well. I think I expected praise for being adventurous.

It didn't take me long to hate being in my house alone. I was tired of seeing the pictures hung on the walls and the memories we'd never get to make together again. I knew I had to get out. I had to keep my thoughts at bay with a new project.

Even though Chad said to take a few days, I dressed and prepared to go into the office. The sooner we got everything up and running, the more work would be left on my plate, which meant more time I could spend away from my lonely house.

I went through my contacts, setting up an afternoon appointment, which would include the company attorney and accountant. The lawyer firm didn't deal with divorce. I was still too distraught to mentally deal with that kind of permanent fix, so it was a good thing.

Chad would be surprised, probably a little pissed I overstepped, but it was important I made sure I still had a job to go to in the future. I was going to go ahead and get things set up, if he didn't like it he could ream me out later.

After my train ride, and a quick walk to the office, I entered with a set of goals in order. I'd made a plan up in my head, consisting of the amount of employees I'd like to keep for the agency, and a recommendation of qualified individuals who could work on Chad's new project. I wanted to save as many jobs as possible. There were probably going to be a few people who were too bitter to consider returning. They'd been told their job was over. If they didn't enjoy what they did, it was always a perfect excuse to find something else. For the people who invested years with the company, it was the break they needed. They'd be able to provide for their families.

I wasn't surprised the receptionist was on the phone when I walked on. She waved to me, not seeming like my being there was a shock. I headed toward my office, finding it in the same way I'd left it. The conference room door was closed. I wondered if Chad was inside with his grandfather Charles. I was curious to find out if he'd told him about my plan, or if after last night he was going to tell me to find another position at the loony bin.

It took me a while to make some calls and prepare a spreadsheet to go along with my proposal. When I had it all complete I asked the receptionist to have Charles and Chad to meet me in the conference room.

I sat patiently, trying not to picture him naked between my legs. As the thought slipped through my mind, I felt warmth rushing over my body. Then I saw him entering the room, his grandfather following behind him. While Charles was all smiles, Chad seemed to be annoyed. He gave me a once over, while his grandfather came over to kiss me on the cheek. "Rachel, it's good to see you. Chad says you have something you want to talk to me about. I can already tell it's going to be a good idea since it's coming from you."

"I appreciate the vote of confidence. Why don't you let me go over some things? I hope you don't mind, but I've invited Joe Chambers and Kathryn Reston to join us in a bit, provided you want to proceed. We need to act fast, and I'll explain why."

Chad still hadn't said anything. I stood and slid a folder in his direction. He was sitting opposite of me, playing with his phone, as if I was taking away from something.

I tried to ignore him and focus on Charles. I knew how much he loved his company, so the idea of salvaging it would delight him. While I ran through my ideas Chad remained silent. He didn't comment or take notes like I would have. As a matter of fact, he was acting as if he wasn't even in the room with us. At one point he was clearly watching a video on his phone, smiling as something funny happened.

It made no sense to me, but I knew I had to stop worrying about it so much. I knew last night had been a mistake, but I refused to regret it. My painful life needed reprieve and I'd found it with him. So what if he was younger. I didn't care. He was safe, and good at it. I enjoyed it immensely.

Finally, after going through the entire presentation, Charles clapped his hands together. "I think we've got a good plan, Rachel. I didn't think you'd want to take on such a large project, or else I would have suggested it before. I knew I was going to be retiring, and without Chad there wouldn't be anyone willing to put in the time to keep the agency going. This pleases me."

"Good." I turned my attention to Chad. "How do you feel about it?"

He never looked up. "I told you last night it was a great idea."

That was all he would say.

Charles and I had some small talk while we waited for the two individuals to join us. Chad stayed in the room, but said little about anything. He got up and made a few calls in between. I kept looking at him, hoping for a single sign of him glancing in my direction. It happened once for a brief second. My heart began to pound in my chest. I felt butterflies in the pit of my stomach and rush of flashbacks to our rendezvous.

We spent three hours that afternoon strategizing and filling out paperwork for tax purposes to open a new separate entity of the existing company. After the attorney and accountant had what they needed, they left the room. Charles walked them out, leaving me alone in the room with Chad. He was still in the chair across from me. "I think it went well."

"Yep. Congratulations." He stood, placing both hands flat on the table. "I need to get out of here. Next time I suggest you bring your phone with you. You never know when someone is trying to get your attention." He winked and turned to leave the room.

I couldn't run out of there fast enough to fetch my phone and look at it. I don't know what I expected. I figured he was sending me notes about his feelings regarding the plan, but it wasn't anything like that.

The first message was sent as soon as I'd arrived at the office.

I thought we talked about you staying home. – Chad

The next message was sent before the meeting.

You sneaky woman. I'm going to have to punish you for keeping this meeting from me. – Chad

Are you wearing panties? – Chad

On a scale of one to ten, how bad do you want me to fuck you again? – Chad

There was one last message, sent just seconds before I'd picked up my phone.

I can still taste you on my lips. I couldn't pay attention in that conference room, because I kept picturing myself bending you over and fucking you in front of everyone in there. You did good in there. Congratulations. – Chad

I sat back in my chair and tried to calm down. I had to stop thinking about him. It was necessary to keep my business and personal life separate. We couldn't frolic around. It had to be a one-time thing, besides, I still had a mess of a marriage to sort out. Even though I was pretty certain it was over, I still had a bunch of legal matters to tend to. It would take time, and I refused to spend it bent over a conference table.

I put my phone away, determined to ignore Chad and his antics. I had more important matters to deal with.

Chapter 14

I had a ton of paperwork to do and calls to employees to make. It was important to get everyone back into the office, especially when I'd told them to take their clients elsewhere. I needed them to stay with Leviathan, now more than ever. Since I didn't have a reason to rush home, I stayed in my office determined to get most of it done.

Grayson managed to call my direct line at work, and unknowingly I picked up the phone. "Hello."

"Honey, it's me. Please don't hang up."

"First of all, don't call me that. Secondly, I have no reason to want to hear your voice."

"I know what you did last night, and you made your point. We're even. Let's stop hurting each other and fix what's broken. Please, I'm asking you to reconsider. Let me take you out tonight so we can talk. I'll tell you anything you want to know. Rachel, I'm lost without you. Just let me explain. Give me a damn second of your time."

I started to hang up, because I didn't give a damn what he had to say to me, but something stuck out to me; something made me feel sad. He knew I'd been with Chad.

He said we were even. I knew damn well he'd slept with Kyla way more than one time. They'd screwed around for months behind my back, yet I'd been open about Chad staying with me. He didn't know my intentions were honest in the beginning. Chad was only being a friend. "I don't think I can sit in the same room as you."

"I get it, I do, but you hurt me too. God, you took a knife and drove it through my heart last night. Tell me you didn't go through with it. Tell me it was just a ploy to pay me back. Say you didn't sleep with that guy."

"I'm not saying anything to you. I don't have to. You broke our vows. As far as I'm concerned, you ended our marriage. You certainly ended our commitment to each other. What I did with my friend last night is no longer your business. I'm not going to pretend what I did was right, but it was my choice, just like sleeping with Kyla was yours."

"No. This isn't a competition. I'm trying to save our marriage."

I began to laugh at his comment. "It's a little too late, don't you think?"

"Rachel, please. What about counseling?"

"Counseling is for couples who want to be with each other. Was last night not clear for you?"

"You're acting out. In time you'll change your mind. You know you love me. It doesn't go away overnight. It's not that fast."

"Oh really? Let me ask you this then. How long have you been sleeping with Kyla? How long have the two of you been involved?"

The line was dead silent. Then in almost a whisper I heard him reply. "Six months."

"Yeah, it happens that fast." I hung up the phone, feeling more pissed now than before. Six months. He'd been sleeping with her for six months in our house. I wanted to rip my hair out and scream. How could they do it? How could they look at me and pretend they weren't screwing around behind my back? Did they not feel any sort of remorse? I wanted to puke. The bile was rising to my throat so fast I didn't know if I could swallow it back down.

I had to sit still for a few minutes, calming down enough to continue working. A knock at my door was startling. I wasn't in any condition to answer, so when I saw it crack open I freaked out. "Can't you knock?"

Chad came in and shut the door behind him. "Sorry it's just me. I thought you might be hungry, so I ordered enough for both of us." He stopped talking when he saw my face. "What's up?"

I rubbed my temples as I explained. "I just got off the phone with Grayson. He pissed me off, that's all. It's nothing new."

He took a brown bag and slid it across the desk toward me, while taking the seat opposite mine again. He pulled out a box of Chinese and used a fork to take a bite. "Eat something. I know you haven't stopped once today."

He was right. "You don't have to feed me. I'm perfectly capable of taking care of myself."

I opened the bag anyway, starved more than I was willing to admit. What I pulled out was not edible, at least I didn't think so. "What are these?" I said as I held up a pair of panties and matching bra.

"A woman should already know the answer to that question, Rach."

"Why are they in my dinner bag?"

"Oh." He wiped his face and crossed his arms. "Well, I was thinking you might be uncomfortable, I mean, you've been cooped up in this office all day. I figured we could grab a quick bite to eat and then freshen up before we head out."

"Head out? Where would I freshen up at?"

"My place. Yours is too far away. We'll miss the show."

"Show?" I was utterly confused.

"You are a size six, correct?"

I could feel my cheeks blushing. It was sort of silly since he'd seen every bit of me less than twenty-four hours earlier. "Why do you want to know?"

"Well, I'm not going anywhere with you dressed like a private school teacher. It's hot and all, but not cool for tonight."

"Who says I'm going anywhere with you?"

"Do you have something better to do?" I shrugged. "Grayson wanted me to have dinner with him.

We do need to talk."

"True. It's just, I got these tickets to a musical from one of our clients. My grandfather thinks it's good for business if we go to support him, especially since we're keeping the doors open."

"So it's work related?"

"More or less. As the new CEO of Leviathan Agency I figured you'd want to join me. Professionally of course."

I raised my brow, giving him a sarcastic gaze. I knew he was full of himself. After his flirtatious texts earlier, it was obvious he was playing games with me. "You know I have a ton going on."

"I can ask someone else, though, I think I remember you mentioning how much you liked musicals. It's front row, Rach. It's one night. It will give you time to gather what you want to say to your hubby. What do you say? Do you care to join me?"

I was dying to see the show, but when tickets were for sale I'd decided it was too late in the evening to travel on the train. The city wasn't a safe place at night, and I wasn't exactly a huge woman. "Since when have you paid attention to what my interests are."

"Rach, there's a lot more to me than meets the eye. I thought you figured that out last night."

"Last night." I tapped my fingernails on the desk. "Last night was…"

"A mistake?" He stood and shook his head. "I told you it was a bad idea."

I began to playfully giggle. "Were you not in the bed with me? I enjoyed myself, more than I thought I could. I just think we should leave it there. I can't get involved with you. I'm too old for you, and if you haven't noticed I come with a lot of baggage. I don't even know where I'll be from day to day."

"I told you I didn't want a relationship, but if a beautiful woman enjoys my company, and I feel the same, I'm sure as hell going to take advantage of it. I don't give a shit if you're married, Rach. You're stunningly delectable, every damn inch of you. Last night was my pleasure, but I agree with you. We should keep it professional. I'll just return the panties. You don't have to go with me."

"No. I want to go."

"And the panties," he asked.

I pushed my chair away from the desk, standing and walking to the side he sat. I slid my body between him and his food, leaning my ass on the edge of the desk. I held the panties up with one finger in front of him. "You mean these?"

He went to grab them and I jerked them out of his reach. "I don't wear these thong looking things."

"Try them on. At least let me see them one time. Come on, just for a second."

I rolled my eyes and looked at the clock. "People still might be here."

"We're the last two people here. I checked already. Besides, your door is shut. Take off your clothes and give me a show."

"No, you're crazy."

"I like it when you fight. My dick's already getting hard. Do you want to feel?"

Of course he was confident. The guy could have any woman he wanted. I still couldn't believe he was interested in me. I wondered if I was some kind of bucket list challenge for him. Did he plan to gloat to his buddies at the gym, bragging about how he was nailing a married woman? "I thought we agreed this had to stop."

"I don't have a turn-off switch. I get what I want, and what I want right now is you, in those panties, spread eagle on this desk." He patted the flat surface as he said it. "Let me fuck you like I know you've been imagining all day."

I had a choice to make. I could do the right thing and tell him it wasn't a good idea, or I could give in to temptation and have another go at something that was sure to leave me satisfied.

The decision was simple.

Chapter 15

Where was I supposed to change? It wasn't like there was a dressing room, or a personal bathroom in my office. I wasn't that high up in the company, well not yet at least. I held up the tiny amount of fabric. "Right now? You want me to stand in front of you and strip?"

He smirked and nodded. "You're damn right. I want to watch."

I kept trying to see Chad as the kid I'd once known him to be, but after his recent performance, and the way he was such a gentleman, I couldn't look past his true identity. He was strong and powerful, with women fawning over him. I'd be a fool to pass up the opportunity for some cheer-me-up fun, and that's exactly what this was. It meant nothing to either of us. We were two adults, enjoying the company of each other after a hard day. "You ignored me in the meeting," I said as I dropped my skirt to the floor. "Why? If I'm so appealing to you, how come you didn't give me a second's notice?"

"After last night, I can't look at you without my dick getting hard. Unless you wanted a different kind of presentation it was best if I kept my eyes on note taking."

"Note taking. I saw you laughing several times."

"I was laughing when I was messaging you." He pulled out his phone and scrolled to an application before handing it to me. "Take a look for yourself. I had the dictation on, and when more than one person was speaking, I tried to jot down as much as I could. If I needed to go back and reference anything later, I'd have access to it. If you paid any attention to me in our other meetings you'd know I do this every time."

I was shocked. He'd been listening the whole time. "I thought I was boring you."

"Trust me, Rach, nothing about you is boring, you proved that last night, more than once if I remember correctly."

My cheeks turned a crimson hue, I was sure of it. I'd acted on impulse, throwing caution to the wind. I'd done things with Chad I'd never tried before, and I liked it.

I lifted my top over my head, standing before him in only a bra and panties. When I knew he was paying full attention, I unfastened the back clasp and let my breasts fall free. Instinct told me to cover up. I brought my arms up to my shoulders, hiding both nipples from his sight.

"You look like a stripper. Do you have moves to go with it?"

I wasn't the best dancer, but I could shake my ass around to a beat. "There's no music."

"Close your eyes and pretend." I watched him unzipping his pants. As shocking as it was to be doing this in the office, it felt kind of risqué. The idea of it turned me on. Parts of me were tingling, and it was only a matter of time before I was begging him to touch me.

I moved my hips from side to side, keeping my eyes focused on his. Meanwhile, he'd pulled his erect cock out of his trousers and was holding it, moving his palm slowly around it. I tried not to look at it – the size; what had been inside of me earlier. It was hard to keep my concentration as I shimmied out of my panties, suddenly stark naked before him.

He stood, letting go of his shaft and coming toward me. Instead of touching my skin, he reached behind, grabbing the bra and panties off the table top. He stared me in the eyes while putting each strap over my arms, then fastening it in the back. I watched as he crouch down in front of me, face to face with my pussy. He held out the panties and watched me place both of my legs in each slot. Then, as slow as humanly possible, he raised the fabric up until I felt the thong sitting against my ass crack.

Chad stood and backed away, taking me in once more. "Nice. Now turn around. Show me that ass."

I did as I was told, really getting into it. My hips moved side to side as I ran my hands through my newly cut hair.

He spanked me once on the left side, catching me off guard. Then he began rubbing the area, while forcing me to bend over the desk. I could feel his stiff cock pressing against my ass, but I said nothing. I already knew what was coming, and I wasn't about to stop him. I'd fantasized about having sex at the office, but never in my wildest dreams had I imagined it with someone as handsome as him.

I also hadn't pictured myself being with another

man, since I'd vowed to love and cherish my husband for the rest of my life. All that was gone now though.

"I should take you right here, like this, but I'm going to hold out." He spun me around, scooting some items on my desk out of the way. "Climb up there and spread your legs."

I did as he requested, hopping up on the desk and spreading my legs to either side. "Like this?"

"Yeah. Now, run your hands up the inside of your thighs while I get comfortable."

I expected him to approach me, instead he sat back down, grabbing his fully erect cock and began stroking it. Watching him masturbate was turning me on. As much as I wanted him to touch me, I was getting off on the idea of him pleasuring himself to my body.

I kept massaging my thighs, feeling the warmth forming between them. "Are you sure there's no one else here?"

"I watched the last person leave, Rach. Quit worrying and scoot your panties to the side. I need to see that pussy."

I slid the fabric over, watching as I exposed my private area for his viewing pleasure. "Like this?"

He shook his head and grinned. "No, you'll need to use your fingers. Make yourself wet, Rach. Show me how you touch yourself when you're alone. Come for me."

Was he crazy? I couldn't do that, could I? Did I have the courage to do something so taboo with him watching me intently like he wanted to?

I took two fingers, slightly grazing my clit. The mere touch caused my muscles to tighten.

"Wait. Hold on." He tapped on his lips with one finger and stood, getting close enough where he could touch me. He reached forward with both hands, forcing the lace cup of my bra on each side down, exposing my breasts. He backed away, as if to appreciate them like they were a work of art. "Yeah, that's better. Now where were we?"

I couldn't get over how collected he was, letting me know he was experienced beyond his years. He was a powerful man, his age meaning nothing anymore. He besieged me in a way I couldn't yet explain. Whatever he requested I wanted to do.

Inundated with desire, I watched as Chad sat back down in his chair. He left his cock alone and folded his hands together, grinning as he brought his attention to me. "You know what to do. Don't make me wait, Rach. This is just foreplay. You won't be fucked if you don't play by my rules, and we both know you want more of this." He pointed to his groin, smirking the entire time.

I circled my fingers over my clit again, this time applying more pressure. His alluring stare kept me flushed. My heart rate increased, and I felt overheated, even though I knew the temperature in the room hadn't changed. The more I continued, the harder it was to keep focused. When this was over I'd seek absolution. Until that time came, I would bathe in the ecstasy this man was offering.

"Tell me again what I'll get if I abide by your orders?" I managed to get out before having to inhaled deeply. The intensity was building. Friction against my clit sent shudders throughout my body.

"What's the hottest sex you've ever had?"

I tried to think of the most sensual moment of my life. My mind kept going to the night before, and the things Chad had been able to do with his hands and tongue. I knew I couldn't give him anymore reason to think he was amazing, so I tried to think about every single experience I'd ever had. I closed my eyes and focused while still maintaining the same rhythm with my fingers on my clit. "It was when I first met Grayson. He was older, and way more experienced. We'd gone out of town for a business trip. After having one too many drinks we thought it would be fun to see an X-rated movie together. The place was empty except for a few random patrons sitting around the theater. I'd never watched porn, so you can image how insecure I was watching it on the big screen. The sound was turned way up, and it felt like the moans were coming from someone sitting next to us. The plot was about some alien invasion of all women. They had a mission to come to earth and learn physical attributes of human men. The woman would walk around grabbing men off the streets and fuck them in random places. After the first scene I was flustered and totally turned on. Being the only female in the theater, I kept looking around to see if anyone was peering in our direction. Grayson stuck his hand down my shorts and began fingering me. After a while it started feeling so good I couldn't help but want more. The moment I peered into his eyes I could see how hungry he was to fuck. I freed his dick from his pants and started jerking him off. Then I had to have it in my mouth. I blew him in the dark theater with people around us. I didn't even care if they watched us. Halfway through, Grayson made me stop. We stood up and ran out the emergency exit, ending up in the rear parking lot. He pressed me up against the brick building and fucked me. I have no idea if there were cameras. Someone could have been watching us, and it turned me on."

"You like being watched?" He asked.

"Yes," I whispered. "I suppose I do."

"Finger yourself. I want to see how wet you are."

I drove my fingers inside my soaked opening, pulling out natural lubricant and rubbing it over the outer lips.

"I knew it. Now, make yourself come. Show me how long it takes you to get yourself off."

I'd just told him a dirty story. Thinking about it, imagining it in my head, made my pussy pulsate. I looked down, forgetting about Chad for a moment. The only thing important in the room was me, and I was about to lose it. I bit down on my lip, sucking in until I could taste the blood rushing to it. This was it; the moment I was going to lose myself in a self-induced orgasm while Chad stared, captivated by my actions. I glanced up at him, catching his gaze and fell apart, my body going into an immediate spasm. My eyes closed and I cried out, forgetting we could be discovered if someone were still in the office.

Chad remained in the same position. He was smiling, waiting for me to settle. "That was hot. You've got me in quite a predicament, Rach. My dick is rock hard, but I've got a big problem."

"What?" I inquired.

"I'm not sure if I want to fuck you on the desk, or

have you ride me until the sun goes down."

I gasped, my pussy still throbbing from my orgasm. The idea of his being inside of me was an immediate draw. I didn't care where we did it, or what position. I just wanted it to happen as soon as possible.

I rubbed my thighs, moaning softly. "I think you should fuck me here first."

"You'd like that wouldn't you?"

I nodded and licked my lips. He had no idea how bad I wanted him. As shocking as it was, I didn't have to be drunk this time to be sure. I craved to have him fill me, and the longer he made me wait, the hornier I became. "Yes. Please. Make me come again. Make me forget, Chad. Make it all go away."

He wasted no more time with questions. As quick as a rabbit, he came at me, running his hands up over my knees and then to my thighs. His thumbs traced the lower lips, spreading me open while he watched. He nudged his cock into my opening, then finally I felt it, his all consuming huge shaft shoving inside my tight walls. Nothing existed except for the two of us. Chad took me to a place where problems didn't exist. A place where euphoria was accessible.

I was in awe, unable to accept that my actions were sinful. I didn't even care. As long as he kept giving more, nothing could break me.

Chapter 16

She wouldn't speak to me. She refused to see me. My own daughter had shut me out. With nowhere else to go, I decided to check out of the hotel and head home. Rachel may have wanted me to go, but it was my house before we met. If she wanted to avoid me, I'd make it almost impossible for her.

I expected to find her at home when I finally got off work. It was late, and she usually went to bed around nine in the evening. There was no use calling her cell phone. She hadn't been answering when I called, and when she did, her words were anything but pleasant.

After putting my things in our bedroom, I made my way downstairs to the living room. Remnants of her romp with the other man were still present. Two glasses and my empty bottle of bourbon remained on the oak table I'd refinished with my bare hands.

I thought back to then, when I believed nothing could tear us apart. Rachel was always happy. Her smile was like a breath of fresh air. For the life of me I couldn't remember back to when I'd seen it last. My heart ached a little more, reminiscing of the life we once had.

Now in shambles, I was grasping at straws to hang on to whatever was left. I'd been ignorant to her feelings, putting my own wants in front of our needs. We needed each other, that I was positive of. Living separate, imagining a life without her in it made me break down. I was crumbling, determined to do whatever necessary to prove we could get through this, maybe even stronger than we were before.

I stared at the glass I knew was meant for her companion. The idea of him putting his mouth on my wife was excruciating. There were things I swore I'd never do to another person, but damn if I didn't want to retract that view and let the guy have it.

She was mine. Yes, I'd fucked it up. Yes, it had been my fault. Yes, I probably deserved much worse than she was giving me.

I had to keep trying. Giving up wasn't an option when it came to Rachel.

Hours passed, in which I pulled out another glass and filled it to the brim. I needed to alleviate some of the stress I was under. A constant ache had been in my chest since all of this went down, and I wasn't sure if it was my heart, or my mind playing tricks on me.

I don't know how many times I flipped through the channels looking for something to bide my time while I waited for her to come home. I mentally prepared for her guest to come in with her, and how this time I was going to stand my ground and be the last man remaining. I wasn't going to allow some stranger to be alone with my wife in our home.

When I began to drift asleep, I wondered if she was coming at all. It was past midnight, and I hadn't even heard a car go by outside. Then, just as my body began to relax, I heard the garage door opening and a car pulling in.

I sat up on the couch, waiting to be met by my wife, and anyone she might have brought home with her.

Rachel walked in carrying her computer bag. She was dressed to the nine in a formal gown that was tight fitting. She wasn't happy when she flipped on the light switch and found me waiting. "I thought that was your car out front. What are you doing here?" It was obvious she wasn't thrilled to see me.

"I'm worried about you. Why are you just getting home?" The truth was that I needed to know if she'd been with *him* again.

"That's none of your business. I think we've already addressed that. What are you doing here?"

I smirked while throwing up my hands, as if she didn't have the right to question it. "I decided to come home. I'm not staying in a hotel when I have a perfectly good house I'm paying for. You never answered my question. Why are you so late?"

"Not that it's any of your business, but I was at work, and then went straight to a show. One of our clients was performing and gave us free tickets, front row. I had to change at the office." She stepped out of her heels and started walking toward the steps. "I'm tired, and for once I had a fantastic night. I'm not going to stand here and let you ruin it. If you'll excuse me, I have work in the morning. I'm going to bed."

"Rachel, wait." She spun around and gave me a look

of annoyance.

"What?"

"We really do need to talk."

"There's nothing to talk about. I want a divorce, and there isn't a single thing you can do or say to change my mind."

Chapter 17

His words were like a knife driving deep into my heart. "I'd marry you again if I could. We could start over anywhere you wanted. We could put the past behind us, both of us. I know you still love me, Rachel. I can see it in your eyes. It wouldn't hurt so much if you didn't. Please don't give up on us. Don't throw away ten years we've had together. We can make new memories."

I don't know why his words were getting to me. It was as if a barrier was about to shatter, and I wasn't able to fight back. The truth was, I did love Grayson. I loved him with every bone in my body. There were times when I felt like I couldn't breathe without him in my life; that if something ever happened to him I'd die myself.

Maybe I was just tired, or it was possible the guilt was beginning to eat me alive. I could feel the rush of tears falling down my cheeks, and the way my lips were trembling from attempting to hold in my feelings. This wasn't easy, and I certainly couldn't be prepared for how my heart would feel when he sat so close, pleading for me to love him. Even a quick glance to his face told me everything I needed to know. Grayson was telling the truth. He wanted to start over. In a way, I wanted the same things, but my inability to get over his indiscretions left me unable to forgive.

It was possible time would heal my broken heart, but for now I wanted nothing to do with Grayson, and the pain being around him brought me. "I can't. I'm sorry. I know you're trying, but I'm not ready for this. I don't know if I will ever be. It hurts too much." I sniffled to prevent the snot from pouring out of my nose. I had to stay strong. It was important for him to understand I couldn't shut off the images in my mind. They were still fresh and just as painful. "You have every right to be here in your home, but I can't promise I'll be able to handle being around every day. It might be better if I found a small place to rent in the city, at least temporarily."

"Is that where he lives?"

Wow. He had nerve. "What does it matter? Is your office close to your girlfriend's house?" It was a low blow.

Grayson shook his head. "She's not my girlfriend. I told you it's over. I have no intentions of seeing her ever again."

"I guess six months was plenty of time for you to get your fix."

"You're not being fair. What about your new boy toy?" His assumption made me giggle.

"Boy toy? Did you seriously say that?"

The funny part was that Grayson should have recognized Chad. He'd met him quite a few times at holiday parties. Chad had changed a lot since then. He was older, and much more mature, but he still resembled the same person.

"Yeah, I did. He looks like you picked him up from a magazine shoot."

I covered my mouth and giggled. Grayson was jealous. I suppose I could relate. Every time I thought about him with Kyla, I felt like I wasn't good enough anymore. Grayson saw Chad as a threat, and he should have. In two days I'd had more fun in and out of the bedroom with Chad then I could ever remember having with Grayson. My husband was sort of selfish when it came to sex. Chad went out of his way to make each time we were together amazing. I don't know. Maybe I was just excited because it was something new, at a time when I felt like the rest of my life was a huge mess. He distracted me, and also made me feel like I was sexy and attractive. He made it easy to forget I'd been cheated on. "He's a friend and that's all you need to know. I owe you nothing as far as an explanation goes. You ripped me apart. If I enjoy someone else's company, it's your own fault. You did this to me, Grayson. Don't forget it for a second. You set all this into motion, not me. I'm just trying to get by without wanting to give up altogether."

He wept in his hands, unable to look up at me. My heart ached for him. It was obvious his pain could have been diminished had I been caring, yet I wasn't going to budge, not yet anyway. Until I could stop being so angry, Grayson was going to have to deal with the repercussions of his own actions. My extracurricular activities weren't his concern. Maybe in some ways I was doing it to get back at him, but when I thought about today's actions, I wondered if it was more about me wanting something I'd never had before; something Grayson had never been able to give me.

I sighed, feeling like I was making his pain worse, and sat down beside him. "A part of me will always love you. We will need to get along for Stephanie. She'll want to spend holidays together. I need time to heal so I'm able to do that. I'd like to be able to be in the same room and not want to strangle you. Right now it's still too painful. I've never felt so alone as I did when I saw you with Kyla. I trusted the both of you, and you took me for a fool."

He tried to reach for my hand before I pulled it away. I stood, unable to allow him to try again. "Rachel, don't give up on me."

"I have to go to bed now. I've got a busy day tomorrow. On top of everything you put me though, I almost lost my job. I was home early that day because we got word the company was closing it's doors. Charles is retiring and his family wants to pursue other ventures. I needed you, and come to find out you were here fucking a child we'd thought of as family. Speaking about it makes me sick." I turned my gaze away from him. "I have an opportunity to save the company, but it's going to take a lot of time and I've already committed to it. Tomorrow I'll search for a small place to rent. I get how much it hurts you. It's killing me too. You think I wanted to see this happening between us? I wanted to be with you forever. When I said those vows I meant them."

"I know," he replied sadly. "I'm sorry about your job."

"Like I said, I think I can save the company, and even better my position. I met with Charles and his grandson today. We brought the lawyer and accountant in, and went over the numbers we'd need. We're going to have to move to a smaller facility, and half the staff will still be without jobs, but it's a start. I'm hopeful I can keep a lot of people who need their jobs to support their families. I've got a lot to do, and I know if I throw myself into this, I'll be able to get by day to day without you in my life. I won't be happy. There's nothing I want more than this to all go away. It's just not feasible. I'm asking you to give me time. I can't offer anything else."

He nodded, even though I could tell he wasn't thrilled with my decisions. "Okay. I can give you time. Just promise me you won't meet with a lawyer, not until we talk again. Promise me you won't take drastic measures when it comes to our marriage."

It was a fair request. "Okay. I promise I won't see the lawyer yet."

I started walking up the stairs and heard him coming up behind me. "Rachel, wait. There's something I need to say, in case you're gone when I get up."

I stopped and gave him my attention. "I'm listening."

"This new guy, whoever he is. I hope he's what you need. You're right. I have no business asking you what your intentions are, but that doesn't mean I don't still care. If this is what you need to cope, I get it. Some people won't, but it makes sense. You need to do this, because I've made you feel like you weren't enough for me. I promise I've never felt that way about you, but I get you need to do whatever it takes to get through this. If you ever need to talk please know I'm here for you. I always will be. No matter how long it takes you to see it. I'll be the man waiting for another chance. I love you that much, Rachel. I'd give you to someone else if it helped you heal." He was breaking down in front of me. I felt horrible. "Just know he'll never love you, not the way I do. One day you'll believe that. I just hope I'm still around when it happens."

I ran up the stairs like my feet were on fire. I had to get away from him. Grayson knew me too well. He was going to say whatever he could to get into my good graces. He was willing to throw himself under a bus to make me see how much he was willing to sacrifice to get me back.

A part of me felt appreciative, while the other half of me still wondered if I'd ever be able to look at him as anything but the cheater who ruined our lives.

In all my efforts to remain calm, his words crushed me. I locked the bedroom door and sulked. While some would find comfort in knowing they had someone to wipe away the tears and make them forget, my heart still remained with my husband; the man I'd built a beautiful life with.

Sure, in some ways I'd made the same choices, yet I never would have gone in that direction had he not done it first. I'm not justifying what I was doing as the right choice for everyone. For me personally, it was the only way I saw myself being able to get over his betrayal. I could now understand how easy it would have been to fall victim to my own desires. I'd slept with Chad for a few reasons, but mostly because I wanted to forget about my problems and feel good about myself again.

For the most part it was working, except for when I was alone, like right now. I looked around the room, thinking about the time we'd spent the weekend repainting the walls, or when Grayson decided to surprise me with new bedroom furniture. On the walls were pictures we'd purchased when we'd taken a family trip to Guanacaste

Costa Rica when Stephanie was just eleven years old.

The Vase on my nightstand was purchased on a trip to Canada we took as chaperones when Stephanie was in the marching band and there for a competition. Our bedding was from the Amish market, and the matching curtains Grayson had made for a birthday present.

Everywhere I looked were the memories of our beautiful life. Everything I touched reminded me of it, like the sheets we'd bought on sale when a local store was going out of business. They were soft, and inviting, and when I climbed in at night I was so comfortable I fell right asleep.

I already missed our life together. Even with Grayson downstairs it would never be the same. He'd never hold me in his arms and make me feel like the luckiest woman on the planet. He'd never greet me with a welcome home kiss that would make me weak in the knees. He'd never be the person I wanted to share special moments with.

I'd been pushed away by a force so strong it was impossible to forget. Betrayal is ugly. It shows it's face like vicious prey looking to kill it's next meal. It doesn't pick and choose it's victims. We did that on our own. We make the choices that set our lives into a whirlwind of regret. We choose to let the people we love down. Our terrible decisions impact the ones we love the most.

I didn't know how to overcome it, and I wasn't sure if I had the courage to stick around and try.

Chapter 18

Rachel was right up the stairs from me. This was the longest we'd been in the same place since she'd discovered my infidelity. At least I knew she was safe, even if it was from herself. The identity of her special friend didn't matter to me. Of course I was apprehensive about giving her free reign to seek out some kind of resolution, however it was what she sought out to do. No man wants his wife, the love of his life, to be with another man. The idea of it made me sick to the point where I wondered if I'd ever be able to touch her the way I used to without imagining someone else's hands on places only I was supposed to have access to.

I finished off another drink before getting it in my head that going upstairs was a good idea. Once I hit the first step I didn't hesitate. I knew I wasn't going to give up until I was in the room with her.

I didn't knock, or make her aware I was coming in. I simply pushed open the door and found her in bed, sitting on her computer. My side was still folded. I closed my eyes and thought about what I'd done in the bed, and what she'd done with someone else. We'd hurt each other. On my part, there was no excuse. I'd made poor choices, and now had to pay the ultimate sacrifice. "Rachel," I whispered her name softly as I approached the bed.

She closed the screen on her device and stared wide-eyed. "You can't be in here."

Hot tears fell down my cheeks. "Please don't. Don't push me away."

I watched her lids close, and when she opened them back up they were red and filled. "Grayson, I can't do this right now. I thought I explained that."

"I can't let you slip away. I need you. I need you so damn much it's killing me inside. I know I did you wrong."

She threw up her right hand. "You have to stop this. I can't stand it. It's making the situation worse."

"No, you moving out on me is the worst. I'm begging you, let me stay in here. I don't want to be alone. I need my wife. If this is the last time we're ever going to be together, please let me stay in here with you. Give me that, Rachel. Let me be next to you."

She opened her mouth, but closed it before any words came out. I could tell she was confused about how to respond. "Nothing is going to happen between us."

I interrupted. "I know. I'm not even going to try. I just want to be close to the only woman I'll ever love. You might not believe it, but I mean it with all I have left in me. You know me better than anyone, Rachel. Look into my eyes and see how sincere I am. I'm not lying to you. I made that mistake already. I won't do it again."

She scooted over, further than she actually needed to. "Fine. If you try to convince me to change my mind I promise I'll take my things tonight and leave. I'm doing this out of the kindness of my heart. This doesn't mean I forgive you at all."

I walked over to my side of the bed and climbed under the covers, keeping a good distance between us. Rachel opened her laptop and pretended to act like I wasn't close to her. I tried to remain quiet, but being so close to her was causing me to get overemotional. She was my beautiful wife, and I couldn't touch her. My own self-inflicted prison was killing me. "I like your hair," I said softly under my breath.

She turned and looked and me. "I thought you said to never cut it."

"You're beautiful no matter how you wear your hair, Rachel. I've felt that way since the moment I first laid eyes on you. Do you remember the day we met?"

"Of course." She closed her computer lid again. "I'll never forget it."

"I wish we could go back. I know it's not possible now, but I'd do things differently."

"I believe you, Grayson."

"You do?" I shifted to turn my whole body to face hers.

"I'm not oblivious to what you're going through. I have compassion. I can tell when something is bothering you, and it's obvious you're struggling. I am too. This isn't how I saw our future going." She wiped her eyes. "I thought we'd be together forever. I thought we were best friends."

"We still can be."

She shook her head. I watched her face scrunch as she began to weep. "I wish we could. I do. I wish we could make it all go away, but it's too late. Some damage is irreparable. We can't fix what's broken. We've both made choices we aren't proud of. I don't want to hurt anymore. I don't want to feel like this."

I reached over and touched the back of her hand. She started to jerk it away, but at the last minute left it to remain. "Can I hold you?"

She sniffled and shrugged her shoulders. "It will probably make matters worse."

"I don't care. Let me hold you. Please, Rachel."

She leaned over and let me wrap my arms around her. In that moment I lost it. I didn't let go, but I was struggling to keep enough composure to do it. This was it. This could be the very last time I was this close to my wife. This could be the last time I got to hold her; to touch her in any way.

Together, we cried, letting the pain flow out of us like a running faucet. We'd gotten so caught up in our lives that we'd forgotten how to be married. Life was comfortable, and the monotony left both of us vulnerable. Rachel didn't deserve to be cheated on. It wasn't her fault I made the decision to sleep with someone else. The choice had nothing to do with her at all.

Whatever she was involved in now was a direct result of what I'd put her through. She was lashing out, desperate to feel a connection, since I'd ruined our relationship. My self-conscious wife needed to be reminded how amazing she was, and she felt getting the attention from someone else was the best way to do so.

My aching heart wasn't going to heal, not without her in my life. That's why I couldn't bear to think about when morning came and she asked me to leave her alone again.

If I knew anything about my wife it was that she tried to keep the peace. If she was giving in to my requests it meant she was exhausted. She needed reprieve and this was her way of saying goodbye without the words. I could sense it in the way she cried, how much this hurt. Her pain radiated through me as if we were electrically connected. "I'm so so sorry, babe. God, what have I done to us? What have I done?"

I believe every man has a breaking point. Mine was losing Rachel. Being this close to her again brought so much into perspective. I wondered how I would go on without her. The saying is true. You don't know what you've got until it's gone.

Chapter 19

I'm not sure why I agreed to let Grayson back in our bed. The same goes for him holding me. I knew it wouldn't help, but to some degree it made the pain a little easier to bear. He was with me, alone, and in those moments nothing else in the world mattered.

Our temporary fix left me vulnerable again. I found myself questioning if I'd be able to forgive him and start over. There were so many reasons I wanted to trust my husband, but only time would tell if I'd truly be able to. Right now I knew he wasn't seeing Kyla. That didn't mean he wouldn't have a change of heart. I had to wait it out, and in the meantime I had to get my affairs in order, just in case.

With that being said, there was still the topic of Chad. Being close to Grayson made me more aware of the taboo things I'd done with another man. I knew it was important to focus on my job, instead of the little romps we'd been having. At the end of the day I had to live with all my decisions, good and bad.

The next morning I woke up in the arms of my husband. I would have liked to think all the bad was just a dream, but as I sat up and saw my suitcase I knew I was mistaken. My marriage was in shambles, and I was now part of the reason. Grayson was a mess, and my leaving wasn't going to make it any easier, not for either of us.

I tried to sneak out of his reach without waking him, but failed miserably. Grayson stirred, opening his eyes and becoming alert to our situation. "Where are you going?"

"I have to get ready for work. Go back to sleep."

He sat up straight and looked around the room, finally stopping at my full luggage. I watched his face fall to a sad frown. "I was hoping you'd change your mind."

I sat on the edge of the mattress. "I know. I think we need time apart, Grayson. Maybe it will help us."

"Or maybe it will break us apart forever. Last night helped. You have to admit it."

"Last night was intense, yes, but it didn't solve anything. We're still in the same predicament, and without some separation I'm afraid we'll have resentment. We've both made decisions which impact our future. I need to be able to grasp everything before I can handle and decide what comes next. Do you understand?"

He put his head down and traced the fabric of my nightgown. "I love you so much. I just don't want it to be over."

"Grayson, I can't make promises right now. I know it hurts. Trust me, I feel it too. It's just best if we spend time apart."

"You're punishing me. I get it."

"No!" I defended. "It's not about that. We both

need a breather."

"Does your breather have a name?"

This annoyed me. I was trying my hardest to be considerate. This had nothing to do with Chad. I'd made the decision to stop our tryst. I knew what was at stake, and no one, not even Grayson, wanted it resolved as much as I did. "You would go there. Just remember you're the one who made this ugly. I was really hoping we could do this cordially."

I got up and headed for the bathroom. "Come on, Rachel. You can't be serious. I have a right to ask."

Twirling around, I gave him a look of disgust. "No. You don't! You lost your right to my private life. Now, last night opened my eyes to a lot of things, but it changes nothing. I'm leaving. I'm taking some items with me I'll need. Maybe I'll stop by on the weekend for more. I don't know yet. For now, I don't have a set plan. When I get it figured out, you'll be the first to know."

I could tell he wasn't thrilled with my decision, not that I gave a shit. My give a damn had been broken since he screwed Kyla.

"I told Stephanie," he managed to get out before I could close the bathroom door. "She knows what I did, and who I did it with. She refuses to speak to me."

I came back into the room and stared at him, shocked he'd told our daughter about his affair. "What happened? Did she freak out?"

He began to sob, and in an immediate response I

leaned over and touched his shoulder. "She hates me. I'm sure of it. How could I have been so stupid? How could I make such a horrible mistake?"

"Steph loves you, Grayson. I'm sure she's upset. It's not every day your father sleeps with your best friend behind your back. She's in shock. Can you blame her?"

He shook his head. "No. I don't blame her. I just want my family back. Every day it feels like we're falling apart more. I keep hoping time will heal us, but what if it doesn't? What if I've lost both of you?"

"I can't speak for our daughter. What you did destroyed me, but I'm not bitter. Even if we don't get back together, I won't hate you. I may be angry, but you will always be important to me."

He clung to me for a second while weeping. I felt so bad for him, but at the same time I knew if I stayed I'd cave and never forgive myself. This was no longer about teaching Grayson a lesson. He'd been hurt, and I wasn't into rubbing it in his face. I needed space for myself. I needed to know I could forgive him ,because if I couldn't there was no reason to try. "Please don't leave me, Rachel. I'll do anything. I'll go to counseling. I'll go to meetings for sex addiction. I'll do whatever it takes."

"I appreciate that. Let's try this first."

He wouldn't answer me. I let him hold me for a few more minutes before locking myself in the bathroom. I sank to the shower floor and broke down, silently letting my tears wash away. This was too difficult. All of it. I wanted a mulligan, but would settle for a Xanax.

I took my time in the bathroom hoping he'd not be in bed when I came out. I wasn't surprised to find him gone, but could hear he was still downstairs. The sound of the television let me know he was in the living room. I dressed quickly, making sure I had everything I needed for at least a week away from home. I had every intention of looking for a place to rent. For the time being, I'd check into a hotel close to the office. It would save me on transportation costs while I found something suitable.

Carrying my bags past Grayson was difficult. He sat on the couch watching me, but never offered to help. I guess in his own way it was like a slap in the face. He wouldn't assist me in leaving him.

He was still a wreck when I finally said goodbye. I considered hugging him, but knew it would make matters way worse. Once I pulled out of the garage and onto the road a rush of relief hit me. Even though I knew Grayson was suffering, I was happy to be away from it. I couldn't let his emotions guide me to make quick decisions. For me personally, I needed freedom to be able to come to terms with the direction my life was headed.

The office was a ghost town when I arrived. I'd driven my car all the way to D.C. since I knew I'd be staying somewhere. The receptionist wouldn't be in until nine, and I was determined to get some work done before everyone showed up.

I rounded the corner to my office and found an envelope with my name on it. I looked all around, but saw no one. It wasn't until I went inside that I opened it. In fancy handwriting and read the words.

Rach,

Last night was great. Thanks for keeping my company. I know you're going through a lot right now, so if you need a shoulder, I'm your man.

- Chad

I folded the paper and tucked it in my desk drawer where no one would see. Then I rubbed my temples and thought about the previous night.

After our office romp, Chad took me to dinner. We shared a bottle of wine while eating French Cuisine. Then we went to the show, where the front row provided us with a spectacular view. Afterwards, we walked around for a bit, talking about life and the company. Chad had plans for Leviathan, and I appreciated him including me in them.

When he was certain my buzz had worn off, he walked me to the train station, not leaving until he watched me board. I waved goodbye as we took off, all the while wondering how in the world we'd gotten to be friends so quickly.

Now I sat reading his short note and wondering when I was going to see him next. Then my mind went to Grayson, and my heart broke again.

I closed my eyes and focused on me instead of them. I was determined to tell Chad I couldn't see him outside of work. It was the right thing to do. My mind was made up.

Chapter 20

By noon I'd sent out over one hundred emails, and made the remainder of calls to the employees I was calling back into the office. Since the majority of people hadn't returned, it was eerily quiet in the building.

A knock at my door startled me, sending me out of my chair with my hand on my heart. "Come in."

Who I suspected to be Chad, turned out to be none other than my daughter Stephanie. She walked right in, not stopping until she was in my arms. "Oh, Mom. I can't believe this is happening."

"I'm sorry you had to find out, sweetie. It's been a rough few days."

"You should have called me. I could have been there."

I did feel bad for not letting Stephanie in on my problems. Since she'd become an adult she was more like a best friend to me. Since I loved her more than anything in the world, I wasn't prepared to break her heart. If I could spare her the pain I would do it again and again. "There was nothing you could have done. It's a mess your dad and I have to fix together."

"I'm embarrassed to call him that. And Kyla, oh my god don't even get me started. How could she? I mean, how long was she trying to get with him? It makes me sick. She was always trying to spend the night. Do you think it's been going on longer than they say? Could this have been happening since we were minors?" She shivered and shook her body around. "I can't even think about it without feeling sick to my stomach."

I was trying to put myself in her shoes. Sometimes, her inability to understand was because of her age. However, in this situation I felt like she was in the same boat as I was. We were both losing people we loved. "I believe your father when he says it's only been going on for six months. Last night we talked some more. Nothing is resolved, but we agreed to take some time apart."

"Are you getting a divorce?" Her question was abrupt and to the point.

I shrugged. "I don't know, Steph. I can handle a lot of things, but this, I'm just not sure I can ever get over it."

She frowned and turned her head to look away. I could tell it was because she was getting upset. I reached for her wrist, catching her attention. "You're not going to lose me. No matter what, I'm always going to be your mother."

She hugged me again, this time while sniffling. I needed this kind of embrace, especially after the night I'd had.

A quick knock followed by someone speaking sent our eyes toward the door. "Hey, are we doing…" Chad met my daughter's gaze and smiled, quickly stopping his sentence before there were questions to be asked. He scratched his head. "Sorry to interrupt. I didn't know you had company."

"It's fine," I managed to say with a smile.

"Are we still doing that conference call at three?"

I knew there was no conference call. Chad was giving me a way out of the curious look my daughter was giving us. "Yes, it's all set up."

He tapped on the door frame. "Cool. Ring my office when you're finished so we can go over details."

Once he disappeared Stephanie turned around and gave me a once over. "Who was that? Holy crap he's hotter than hell. Why have you been hiding him from me?"

Of course she'd want to know more about Chad. Every woman did. If it wasn't his fit physique, it was his sugar-bowl dimples, or his bright white smile. It didn't hurt when he opened his mouth and spoke with his gruff voice. "That's the new owner of the company. His name is Chad Rollins."

"Mom, don't hold out on me. Is he married? Single? Is he gay?"

I started to nod, but knew I couldn't lie to her in that way. If she ever saw him again she could open up a can of worms I didn't want to come out. "He's a womanizer. Steer clear of that one."

It was the best I could do without giving away the rush of jealousy I was feeling imagining him having more in common with my daughter than myself. In the past week my views of Chad had changed. I didn't want to have to share his attention with someone else, especially Stephanie.

"That's a shame. He looks like he'd be a real good time," she snickered when she said it.

I slapped her lightly on the shoulder. "Stephanie, you should be ashamed of yourself."

"What? I'm a grown woman. I'm not naïve to what goes on between men and women. I have a little experience myself."

I put my hands up to my ears to muffle the sound. "Stop it. I can't hear this right now."

She giggled and removed my hands. "Let's get lunch."

"Wait. Aren't you supposed to be at school?"

"I had an eight o'clock class this morning. I'm off for the rest of the day. Come on, Mom, don't you miss me?"

"Of course I do. We can go to lunch. I'd love to spend time with you."

Then I stopped dead in my tracks. I'd emailed an agent about seeing two apartments close to the office. I wasn't sure Stephanie would be prepared for that type of move from me. "Wait. There's something I need to tell you."

"What?"

"I made an appointment to look at a couple places to rent." I waited for her to respond.

It was obvious she was hurt by me making such a move so soon, but I wasn't changing my mind. I needed to clear my head. I required time to let it sink in. It was important to be able to forgive Grayson, no matter how long it took.

"Wow." Her demeanor changed. "I guess I didn't expect it to happen so soon."

"Sweetie, for now it's temporary. We need time apart, and instead of spending a ton of money on hotels, I'd rather have a place closer to work to call home. It's not forever." In all honesty, I didn't know if I'd ever live with Grayson again. Only time would tell if we could patch things up.

"I get it. I know it's impossible to face him. I feel the same way. Looking at places seems so real though. I don't know what else I expected. You deserve to be happy, I just always assumed it would be with my father. This makes me sad."

"I know. Me too. Let's hope we all find resolution soon."

"I do." She clapped her hands together. "Well, since I'm here, do you mind if I tag along? I mean, I'd like to be able to come spend the night, so of course I need to have a say in which place you choose."

"It's only two or three properties. It's hard to find something on the spot, especially in the city. People have waiting lists. It's crazy."

After agreeing she should be a part of my decision, Steph and I headed out to look for the new apartment I'd be living in.

The first two places were one bedroom units. The kitchens were small, but manageable. The second one had an additional bedroom. It was one-hundred more dollars a month, but worth it to know Steph would have a place to stay when she visited. It also gave me room to have a home office without making the living room area cluttered. Sometimes my paperwork could get out of hand, and I knew with the new position I'd be bombarded with take-home work.

I wrote a check for the down-payment, and waited as she called a company they used for a credit check. When I left, three hours later, I had the keys to my new place. It wasn't furnished, but at least I had something to call my own.

Stephanie didn't come back to the office with me. We said our goodbyes on the street outside before I headed in to get caught up. I'd no sooner walked in my office when Chad whisked in the room, closing the door behind him. "Who was that?"

"My daughter, why?"

"Your step-daughter?"

"Yes, why?"

"She's cute."

I crossed my arms and leaned back in my chair. "Did you come in here to try and make me jealous?"

He leaned his palms down on my desk and came forward so our faces were closer, but not nearly enough to touch. "No. Why? Are you jealous?" "You're making me uncomfortable."

"Maybe that's my goal. When you're uncomfortable you put up your imaginary guard. I like breaking it down."

I folded my hands together on the desk. "About that. We need to stop messing around, Chad. It's making me feel terrible. I've got a lot on my plate, and this is confusing me. I need to be able to focus on everything else."

"I get it. It's cool. We can be professional acquaintances again. Just because I've seen you naked doesn't mean I can't act normal around you. Sure, I'll never forget the way you smell, or how you taste when my tongue is soaked in your pussy juices, but hey, nothing lasts forever."

The mere mention of him doing that to me got me flustered. Immediately, I wanted to retract my statement and let him bend me over so he was able to fuck me into Sunday. When I was with Chad everything disappeared. I didn't have struggles in my life, because I was temporarily overwhelmed in ecstasy.

"What did you want earlier?"

"I wanted to eat." He corrected. "Food. I was hungry for lunch and wanted a companion to join me. I didn't mean to interrupt."

"I had to go look at apartments."

He raised his brow. "Really? Did you find anything close?"

"Actually, I found a two bedroom off the bypass. It's

over by that pizza place your grandfather likes to order from."

"No shit? I live a couple blocks from there."

"You don't live with your grandfather?"

"Hell no. I just stay there a lot. They have more amenities, like the pool, hot tub, sauna, gym."

"I get it. I've been there before." His grandfather lived in a beautiful mansion. I expected Chad to stay there until he inherited the property.

"Yeah, it's nothing huge. It's enough for me, and it's close to work. Plus, I have a garage to keep my car in."

"A garage. Impressive. I don't even have a couch."

Chad paced around the room and finally turned to face me. "How's the tax situation coming along?"

He was turning our conversation into a professional matter, instead of personal. "It's good. I think by next week we'll have some permanent papers to sign. Are we still good with the same plan?"

"Why wouldn't we be?"

"Well, I've told you I can't be with you again. I didn't want you to get bitter about it."

"Jesus, Rach, I'm not an asshole. You're going through hell. I get it."

"Thank you. I didn't want to have to worry about something else."

"We're good. So, how about some dinner and a bit of couch shopping?"

"I need to save up some money before I buy furniture."

Chad reached in his back pocket and pulled out his wallet, chucking a plastic card in my direction. "Get whatever you want. It's the business account. You can pay it back in payments out of your checks. If you don't, we'll use it as a business expense and write it off."

"What? I can't do that."

"I own the company. Don't make me force your hand."

I rolled my eyes and grabbed the card. "Fine." "Good. Now, what would you like to eat? I'm fucking starving."

"I don't care. Let's do something close to our places. I might not have furniture, but I'll pick up some blankets and sleep on the floor until it's delivered."

"No you won't. You can stay with me."

I shook my head. "Absolutely not."

"Why? Are you afraid you can't resist me?"

I nodded. "Yes, actually that's exactly what I'm afraid of."

He chuckled and sat half his ass on my desk. "I'll keep my hands to myself, Rach. You can have the bedroom. I'm cool with the couch. I usually fall asleep there anyway.

Seriously. It's not a big deal."

"What about the girls you bring home? Don't you need the bedroom?" I was fishing for him to admit he was a manwhore. He seemed to find me hilarious.

"The girls I bring home? Didn't you just say we couldn't be physical?"

I nodded.

"Yeah, well I'm pretty sure I can hold out for the time it takes for your furniture to be delivered."

He wouldn't admit there were other women, and a part of me didn't even want to know the truth. It might make me feel terrible about my decision to sleep with him. "Fine, but only because it's close to work and you have furniture and dishes."

"How about we go shopping, then pick something up to take back? You can change into something comfortable and relax for a change."

"That sounds nice."

"It's settled. Close up your computer and let's get going."

Chapter 21

Work wasn't keeping my mind off of Rachel. I kept contemplating calling her and begging her to come home, but I knew she was getting annoyed. I couldn't continue to push her. She needed time, and I had to give it to her. This wasn't something I was able to rush. I had to give her ample space if I ever wanted her back in my life. Time would be the only factor when it came to our marriage. I was going to have to pray I didn't lose her forever, but if I had, I'd need to learn how to survive without her constant love and support.

Around lunchtime my receptionist told me my daughter had dropped by. Without a second's thought I told her to send the girl straight back to my office. When the door opened I didn't even look up, since I assumed it was Stephanie.

Kyla leaned against the door. She was wearing some low cut number, which actually made her more flat chested than she was. It didn't do a thing for her, though it was obvious she thought she looked amazing. "So, it's been a couple days. I figured you might be missing me."

I pointed to the door, shocked she'd showed up and got through the necessary departments to locate me. "Turn back around and get out. You aren't permitted here, and even if you were, I wouldn't want to see you. Why can't you get it through your head? There is no us. I love my wife.

That will never change. She's my soul mate. She's the reason I want to continue living."

I could tell she was hurt by my words, not that I cared. She'd done this to herself. "I don't believe that. If you loved her so much then why were you with me? Why were your hands on my body instead of hers?"

She had a valid point; one I'd been asking myself since this had been discovered. "I don't know. All I can tell you is that it has nothing to do with feelings. I don't love you, and I will never love you. They are the only facts I have. Frankly, I don't give a damn if you believe me or not. The next call I make will be to the police to have a protective order put out against you. Get it through your thick head, Kyla. There is no us, and there never was. Furthermore, there never will be. You were a cheap screw. That's all I will ever see you as." I motioned for the door. "Find your way out. We're done here."

I was tired of her immature games. She needed to get the hell out of my life and stay away.

As soon as I was able to take a break, I headed to the local sheriff's department to see about the protection order. I was done hoping she'd leave me alone. I needed to make sure it never happened again.

A good hour later I walked outside feeling like I'd accomplished something great. She'd be served papers, thanks to a quick push from an old buddy of mine who still worked for the force. Back when I'd delivered parcels, he'd been one of my regular customers. He'd always included me in fantasy football leagues, and occasionally we'd have a beer. This time I needed his help for something more serious, and he was happy to oblige, but only after I explained my reasoning. Admitting what I'd done to my marriage was difficult to do. Halfway through I felt like I was going to lose my shit in front of him. I managed to keep it together, even after I explained Rachel had moved out.

Before I pulled away from my parking spot I took out my phone and called Rachel. "Grayson, it's not a good time."

Of course it wasn't. There would never be one. "I'll make it quick. I'm changing my phone number. I'll text you from the new one. Kyla will no longer be a problem in our lives. I've made sure she isn't to come within five-hundred feet of us."

"I'll believe it when I see it. I have a feeling she's just getting started. Apparently you're a hard man to forget."

"Is that coming from experience?"

In the background I heard someone speaking and then her laughing. "Sorry, Grayson. I'm in the middle of something. I need to call you back later."

Before I could respond she'd hung up.

I wondered if she was with *him*. I hadn't heard her laugh in a long while. As delightful as it made me feel, I also knew there was someone entertaining her; possibly the same guy she'd had at the house. Fear swept over me. I didn't know what to do. I couldn't accuse her of something, because she'd be pissed. I didn't even think I had a right to. Hadn't I caused this to happen? Hadn't my infidelity been the culprit to begin with?

The downward spiral I was on didn't seem to be slowing down. No matter how hard I tried to stay afloat, I was drowning in my own misery. Without a paddle to fight my way free, I was afraid I'd hit rock bottom.

Chapter 22

"What about this one?" I ran my fingers over the soft microfiber material of the sleeper sofa. "I wouldn't need a bed if I got this one."

"You need a bed. This one is nice. It's comfortable, but if you get the futon for the spare bedroom you won't need a third bed. Get something you love and stop staring at the price tags. Like I said before, it's my treat."

"You and I are partners. I'm not letting you buy my furniture."

"It's a business expense. I won't need to buy new furniture for the business, so this helps me." He directed my attention to another set in the far corner. "That's more your style."

I acted like it wasn't, because him knowing my tastes made me uneasy. "It's ugly."

He cackled something under his breath, took my hand and drug me over until I was plopped down on the fat cushion. "It's perfect."

I went to look at the price and he smacked my hand away. "Stop it. Do you like it or not?"

I shrugged. "Either way you're going to make me get it aren't you?"

"Unless you want to be roommates with me indefinitely?"

As annoying as he was, he had a point. "Fine. I'll get this and the chair. I don't need the loveseat. It's too big."

"Good choice. What about the memory foam mattress? Is that a definite?"

"What? Are you crazy? It's outrageous."

"It's yours. Trust me. Once you sleep on mine, you will want one for yourself."

"Are you sure you don't want to sell things for a living? You're pretty darn good at it."

Chad smiled, taking my hand and bringing it up to his face. He ran his lips over it, but never really kissed it. "Let's get the paperwork done on this stuff. I'm starving."

It took a bit of time to get things ordered, but once we were finished we stopped for a drink before heading back to his place. At first I thought he was trying to get me drunk, but seemed fine when I ordered a non-alcoholic beverage.

Chad sat across from me, sipping on a cold beer in a frozen glass. "Ah, that hits the spot."

"I forgot you were old enough to drink," I teased.

Beyond the glass I saw his amused grimace. He sat his drink down and licked his full lips. *The things he'd done with those lips.* "It bothers you, doesn't it? My age gets to you."

I shrugged. "I guess a little bit. Doesn't it bother you?"

"Younger men like older women. It's not a big deal at all to me. I've messed around with women older than you. It was all in fun."

"Oh," I questioned. "So you do this often?"

"No. I've just had my fair share of experiences. I know what I like. I'm particular."

"I've seen the type of women you like."

"Actually, you haven't. The girls I bring to parties aren't who I spend my time with outside of fancy schmancy events. I like women with intellect. I prefer someone who is equal to me rather than inexperienced."

"So who are the women you bring around to events?"

He smirked. "Promise you won't laugh?"

"I guess."

"I bring them around because secretly my grandfather is a closet pervert. He gets such a kick out of slutty women. Most are my friends from college. They do it for a free night out. We have a good time together, and I don't have to worry about them trying to steal my shit. The last real girlfriend I had was a school teacher. She taught seventh grade English and had a four year old son. She was divorced, and looking for someone to take over the roll of daddy. I wasn't ready for that type of commitment, especially with what's going on in the business. Maybe if the timing was different I could have devoted more time to the relationship, but it's better it ended. She needed someone who worked a nine to five shift. That's never going to be me."

"I thought you were a womanizer."

"Yeah, I get that a lot. Honestly, I don't care. It keeps the gold diggers at bay. I'm picky, and more than anything I don't want my poor grandfather to know I like my women a bit more mature."

Once again my face was flush. "Why are you just mentioning this?"

"You never asked. We aren't exactly a couple. I didn't think it was your business to know. We're friends, Rachel. I have more than one friend. I tell it like it is. Being with you is enjoyable. I like the challenge, and it doesn't hurt that you're fucking beautiful. Do you even know how gorgeous you are?"

"Are you being serious, or joking around?"

"Serious." He reached his hand over and brushed my chin. "It's too bad we can't get freaky anymore. I had high hopes for our next encounter."

Imagining it was all I needed to feel winded. Chad knew it too. He snickered and turned in another direction to hide his amusement. "You're not being very fair. You know I have a ton on my plate."

Chad put his arm around me playfully. "I'm playing

around, Rach. Calm down. I'm cool with us being friends. I'm even cool with you sleeping over, even if we won't be in the same room. I know you're going through a tough time. I shouldn't joke about it. The truth is I want you. I want you more than once. If you change your mind let me know. Until then, I'll be the guy you can turn to. We're associates. We're partners. I know you didn't like me before."

"I never said that."

He laughed. "Yeah right. You never had to. It was blatantly obvious. You hated my guts. You think I didn't notice the looks you gave me?"

I started to giggle. "Okay fine. I thought you were a spoiled prick. That was before."

"Before what? Before I blew your mind?"

I rolled my eyes. "Among other things. Honestly, I think you're a nice guy. I do hope we can be friends. I don't have many of them right now."

"You mean the world to my grandfather. I won't let you down."

I was nervous about staying with Chad, but he was right about being able to sleep in a bed. I had no idea who lived in the apartment before me, and without that knowledge I wouldn't have been able to get any rest on dirty carpet. I'd call in the morning and arrange for it to be cleaned thoroughly before the furniture got delivered.

"Thank you for helping me get some furniture for my place. I was prepared to wait it out until I had the cash." He opened his apartment door and I was shocked. It was like a studio, but I could tell there were more rooms along the walls. Large wooden doors on sliders were hung from some kind of antique looking mechanism.

Chad sat his keys on the granite kitchen counter and started showing me around. "This is obviously where the meals are prepared, when I get a hair up my ass and crave mac and cheese."

I laughed and followed behind him. We came to the living room. He had a video game chair in the center closest to the TV., and a sectional around the rest of the area. "This is where I binge on porn. Be careful sitting. You never know where it's sticky."

When I acted like it disgusted me he shook his head, obviously understanding I took him seriously, when he'd been joking the whole time. "That's where I'll be sleeping, Rach. Your room is over here." I lingered behind him, taking my time checking out everything he'd decorated with. Most of the house was in gray hues. He had black furniture, including his barstools at the counter. His bedroom was exquisite though. A four poster bed sat in the middle of the large room. Layers of fabric were draped at the tops, hanging down each corner. A red comforter was crisply spread across the mattress, with a large amount of pillows surrounding. The dresser and armoire were supersized, and I knew these weren't purchased at a local dealer. "Where did you get this set? It's unlike anything I've ever seen."

"It was my mothers. All of it, including the bedding. It's one of the only things I have of hers, aside from her ashes." He pointed to a fancy urn in the middle of the dresser. "Before she died she made sure my grandparents knew I was to get this. They'd had it stored until I moved out."

"It's amazing," I said as I ran my fingers over the fabric. "It looks brand new."

"I don't sleep with it. When I knew you were coming I had my cleaning lady stop by and change the sheets. The cover always sits folded on the chaise, but when she cleans she puts it on to make it look fancy. I'd hate myself if I ruined it. It was one of my mom's favorite things. She had some lady custom make it."

"It is amazing, Chad. You're sweet to keep it displayed."

"I was a momma's boy. Maybe that's why I have a habit of dating women with children." "Are you sure you want me to sleep in here?"

"Positive. Make yourself at home. I was raised to be a gentlemen. Since you thought I was a douche, it's important I prove you wrong. I can't have you working at my side and whispering to the employees how much of a dick you think I am."

"I wouldn't."

"You would. It's fine. Anyway, I'm just going to grab some of my things and get a shower. You're welcome to stick your bag in the closet if you need more room. Did you want to look at menus while you wait?" He ran out of the bedroom and came back with a handful of them. "Pick what you'd like. I'll be done in ten."

I sat down on the memory foam mattress and started buzzing through the take out menus. Then I heard something that made me giggle. Chad was singing, not just a popular song, but one from the show we'd seen the other night. I held my hand over my mouth and listened for a second before getting up and following the sound to the bathroom. The door was cracked open, and I wasn't prepared for his shower door to be so crystal clear. Most have scum or buildup, but not his. Displaying everything God blessed him with, Chad continued belting out tunes as he washed his hair. I stood there admiring him like a peeping tom. It was terrible, but I couldn't stop. Every inch of him called me closer. I yearned to feel his hands on me again, touching me, and giving me pleasure that took the pain away.

I started to leave, with my hand on the doorknob, but I couldn't take another step. There I was, in his home, standing a few feet from his naked body, and all I could think about was stripping down and joining him.

I shuffled out of my clothes, each article giving me more time to change my mind. Then, standing stark naked before him, I slowly made my way to the large shower door. I placed my hand flat on the glass and watched him turn. The moment our eyes met I knew what I was getting in to. He put his hand up to match mine on the opposing side of the door. It was a silent moment between us. He was connecting with me, telling me it was okay to be scared, resilient, and also eager at the same time.

We said nothing as the door opened and he pulled me inside. Chad stared in my eyes, once again silently communicating with me without the use of words. He wiped the falling beads of water away from my face and leaned forward to kiss me.

I couldn't stop it. I wanted it more than I needed to breathe. "Take the pain away," I whispered.

He pulled my hair back away from my face and brought his forehead to mine. "I remember the first time I ever saw you. You came to my grandparents house for the holiday. I was just a kid, but I could remember how beautiful you were back then. You must have been in your early twenties. I remember thinking to myself someday I wanted to be with a woman as beautiful as you."

I was speechless for a brief moment. My lips parted and Chad placed his against them. "I never told anyone that before, but I wanted you to know it. I've always wanted you to approve of me, not because you worked for the company and I would someday run it, but because you seemed like the perfect woman to strive to impress."

"You're doing a fine job. Don't stop now," I teased.

"Seriously, Rach. Even if you told me to stop, I'd be okay with it, because I got to know parts of you I never thought I would. You think you're weak, but I see you as strong. I might be your distraction. Hell, that's probably all I am. I'm okay with it. I'll be here for as long as you need me to."
"Why?"

"I can't answer that. All I know is, when we're in the same room I need to be close to you. I want to touch you; to taste you. It consumes me. When you're around I feel starved. I know you're forbidden fruit, but I can't help myself. I have to take a bite." He kept stroking my hair as he explained. "Tell me you want me to stop. Say the words and I'll climb out of this shower and leave you alone. Tell me you climbed in here with me because you want to be fucked.

Give me a reason to devour you."

There was no turning around and dressing. I wouldn't be wearing clothes for the rest of the night, and I think we both knew it without a verbal answer. I couldn't help myself. I had to feel his body against mine. "I can give you a million reasons why you shouldn't, but I'm not going to. I can't help myself."

Our lips collided and the world around us disappeared once again. Like a magician, he put me under a spell and I was at his mercy. Nothing could help me now, not even my guilty conscience.

Chapter 23

Chad's touch was like fire igniting across my skin then the flame turning to ice as it made contact. I was burning up and shivering at the same time. I couldn't control my breathing, and as the beads of water fell down my face, I felt his mouth continuously invading my most sensitive of areas.

In order to keep my knees from buckling, I held onto each side of the walls, my head falling back against the hard tile. His tongue, like a battery operated device, lapped at my clitoris, sending me into a flash of jubilation. I was elated with pleasure, overwhelmed by the waves of enjoyment he was providing me.

With each flick, my body reacted with a shudder. His own groans vibrated off my pussy, sending me into an uncontrolled frenzy. I let my hands down and dug them into his thick hair, holding him in place while I screamed out in ecstasy.

My legs were weak, but Chad never faltered. He didn't give me time to recuperate from my first orgasm before plunging multiple fingers deep inside my channel. I almost fell forward, losing my grip on his hair and shaking profusely. His strong arms steadied me, keeping me at bay while he worked his skilled magic. His strokes were patterned, and as his mouth continued to frolic amidst my clit, pulsations whipped over the area. My body was once again convulsing. I'd never experienced such an intense release before. This time Chad lost control over my body. I sunk down to the shower floor across from him, catching his stare as I came to terms with what had just transpired. "Oh my god! Holy shit."

He rinsed his face, using his hands to rub over his five-o'clock shadow. "You said you wanted to forget. How's it going so far, baby?"

When he called me baby my heart fluttered. It was just a term of endearment I found sweet, especially for this scenario. "I think I need a breather."

He fastened his fist around a wad of my hair and pulled me into a deep tongue-filled kiss. I lost myself in it once again, succumbing to the fact that we were only beginning. This encounter was far from over, and I was already panting, exhausted even.

Our intense make out allowed me to climb onto his lap. His huge erection pressed over my bottom, allowing me to anticipate our future events. He paused for a moment, kissing around my neck, while I closed my eyes. "Your pussy is so wet for me. I could slip inside without trying. Damn, I need to have it. I want to take you in my bed and fuck you so unbelievably hard you'll forget anything else exists. For tonight it will just be us, you and me, our bodies connected, your mind clear and relaxed. Say the word and we're there. Tell me not to stop."

"Don't," I abruptly answered. My heavy breathing was pretty obvious. Our tongues met before our lips were able to make contact. His hot breath was against my wet skin again, coursing over the area closest to my mouth. "Please don't stop," I reiterated.

Chad reached up and turned off the water. He scooted over and stood, pulling me up with him. I was dizzy, needing to take a second to regain composure, because parts of me were still tingling. I launched my arms around his neck, awaiting on him to pick me up and carry me out. I didn't have to ask. He attended to our predicament, lifting me so my legs wrapped around his waist. We were soaking wet, slowly moving across the tiled floor.

The temperature changed once we were back in his bedroom. He plopped me down on his soft mattress before joining me, not caring we were still covered in beads of water.

He laced his hands into mine, bringing both down to sit over my breasts. With only his thumbs, he skimmed my nipples, allowing the natural chill in the room to harden them the rest of the way.

I watched his intent-filled eyes ogling each one, before he bobbed down to suck the left nipple into his mouth. I could feel his tongue scour the sensitive tip. My gasps were almost silent, but very able to hear in the quiet atmosphere.

Once again, he grumbled against my flesh, vibrating those tingles to travel to the ends of my limbs.

My body arched, and the heat between my legs intensified, while I struggled to continue holding onto his hands. Finally, he freed them, trailing his fingers down over my hips. It tickled, causing me to shiver. He smiled suggestively, gazing into my eyes as his hand lowered to my pussy. Barely making contact, I felt a slight brushing over the outer lips, before he separated them and played in my wetness. "I might have to wipe you off. You're almost too wet."

"You made me that way."

"Oh, I take all the credit proudly." He walked naked back to the bathroom, coming back out with a rag in his hand. I felt the fabric rubbing over my sensitive origin, doing it's job so we could continue. "Now you're ready."

Chad climbed back on the bed, kissing his way up to my face. He stared me right in the eyes and dove down for a chaste kiss. Then I felt him, his arousal pressing against my opening. The pressure became stronger, and then he was there, fully inside of my channel. I watched his face react to my tight walls. I bit down on my lip and hummed out his name. "Chad, please keep going. You feel amazing."

"You feel amazing, Rach. You like it when I go slow or fast?"

"Both," I managed to say in between deep pants.

"Oh yeah, I know it. You feel so good. Your pussy is strangling me, holding me prisoner. It's so fucking tight I want to come."

"Do it." I was ready. Never in my mind did I consider we weren't using protection. I didn't care. I'd already lost everything. My life was miserable, and this was the only thing keeping me from losing my mind.

"No," he exclaimed while slowing. "I can go all night if we take our time. You need to stop being so sexy."

I crossed my eyes and giggled. "How's this? Does it help?"

He shook his head and leaned down to graze his lips against mine. "No. You're still irresistible. I don't know what I'm going to do with you."

"Just keeping fucking me. Don't stop."

Chad flipped us around, positioning me on top of him. He reached up and pinched both of my nipples at the same time, squishing my breasts together while bringing his face in to lick them. My head fell back and turned into a puddle of lust. I couldn't control my orgasm, as my body bucked above him, I watched him wince and lose himself in pleasure.

Afterwards, we lay there together in the quiet of the room. My head was rested on his chest, while his hands tickled my back. "Let me rest and we'll get back to it."

"We don't have to. This is nice."

"Yeah, it is."

I lifted my head to look at him. "Chad, what are we doing? What is this thing between us?"

"Does it have to be something, Rach? It is what it is. Labeling things makes life complicated. Can't you enjoy what's happening and not question it?"

I shrugged. "I guess. I just have a lot more at stake here."

"Exactly why we aren't going to label this. If you want out, you simply stop. The same goes for me. No complications. No regrets."

I smiled and pretended it was fine, but in the pit of my stomach I felt uncomfortable. This wasn't stable. It wasn't anything more than a convenient fuck partner. We were colleagues. Although it was wrong, I couldn't imagine it never happening again. It was quite a conundrum.

Chapter 24

GRAYSON

I missed her so much. It hurt to get out of bed in the morning. It killed me to walk down the flight of stairs and see the photographs of our family, back when times were happy and we looked forward to spending the rest of our lives together.

I wasn't a fool. I had a feeling she was seeing someone else. Rachel had always been semi- codependent. She needed someone to entertain her needs, especially when she was stressed out.

I knew my wife, so well it hurt, because the truth wouldn't set me free. It would leave me burning away in my own personal hell. Punishment was as easy as looking in the mirror, and there was repentance, not for my sins. I couldn't go back and change the past. My future was gloom and despair. That's all it would ever consist of. Rachel was that one love people search their whole lives for. Unfortunately it took me losing her to see it for myself. She was gone, living somewhere in the city. She hadn't called me in weeks, and that includes returning the slew of messages I'd left on her cell phone.

Stephanie at least had spoken to me a few times. She was always short, speaking more about school than our personal lives. She mentioned staying the night at her mothers and I was glad they had each other, but so damn broken up I couldn't be a part of their time together.

I missed our life, even the bad parts where we had to struggle. I missed their smiles, and the way I always knew they'd love me.

It was gone now. Stephanie couldn't look past what I'd done to our family, not to mention her friendship with Kyla. I think for a while she couldn't believe it really happened. Kyla went to her begging for forgiveness, even throwing the protective order in her face, like I'd done it to spite her. When Stephanie called to ask me about it, I told her everything. I think she believed me, not that she'd say otherwise. Like I mentioned before, she didn't like to talk to me, not about that especially.

Life was getting to be unbearable, but it wasn't until an evening visit that I knew it couldn't get any worse.

A hard knocking was coming from my front door. I called out to hang on, climbed off the couch and went to answer it. Standing on the opposite side was someone I didn't want to face, not now, not ever. Kyla's dad had been considered a friend of mine for years. Now, staring him down in my foyer, I knew there was nothing left of that relationship. "You've got a lot of nerve, serving my daughter with papers after what you've done to her."

"Phil, you need to hear me out. Kyla is out of control. She's stalking me."

"Stalking you? You know what I see, Grayson? I see a grown man who preyed on my daughter. You brainwashed her, forcing her to make decisions she never would have before. Then when you got caught you kicked her to the curb like the trash. This won't stand, Grayson. I won't let

you bring my daughter down with you."
"You've got this all wrong."

"No, I don't think I do."

"So are you hear to take me down? Are you going to hit me? Shoot me?"

Phil stared me down, I suppose to figure out what his next move would be. "I'm here to tell you to drop the bullshit protective order. She doesn't need something like that on her record. You and I both know she's harmless. Don't ruin her life because you couldn't keep your dick in your pants."

This guy had every reason to hate me, but he was wrong. "Phil, your daughter came on to me. She seduced me. It wasn't the other way around. I had to get that order, because she won't leave me alone."

I didn't see his fist coming until it was too late. My nose cracked, and I was certain it was broken. Blood oozed out, pouring down over my shirt, shoes and floor. He pointed to me while I tried to manage the situation. "Stay away from my family, Grayson."

After making sure Phil left, I rushed into the bathroom to access my situation. It was apparent my nose would need to be reset, so I stuffed it with toilet paper and drove myself to the hospital, where I sat and waited for more pain to be inflicted on me.

In that time, I had a chance to think about my life. Without Rachel I was lost. Maybe I deserved the punch. Maybe I deserved everything.

I just wondered how much more I'd have to go through before things would start to look up – or if they'd ever.

Chapter 25

Before I knew it four weeks had gone by. I was only keeping track because that's how long it took for my furniture to finally be delivered. I'd already paid back the money for the living room set. I just owed for a kitchen table and chairs, and my bed, not that Chad cared. He kept telling me not to worry about it, and hiding the money back in places I wouldn't discover until later. For all I knew I hadn't really paid anything back, because somewhere in my things was a wad of cash.

The two of us spent most of our time together, especially after business hours.

I wasn't even that excited about moving into my own place, because I'd become comfortable staying with him.

Stephanie called me every single day. She was adamant about checking on me, although she still had no clue I was having a hot affair with a younger guy. I'd visited her on the weekends when Chad went out of town, and only told her I was staying in the city with a friend until my place was ready. She didn't have a clue I was staying with a guy, especially a sexy younger one I happened to be sleeping with.

Then there was my estranged husband. I hated referring to him that way, but it's exactly what he was. I hadn't seen him in weeks, and I wasn't planning on it anytime soon.

My conversations with him were becoming next to none. I had nothing to say to him, so when he called I had to come up with things to discuss. For the most part he was inquiring about bills I'd normally taken care of. Maybe he just needed a reason to pick up the phone. He sounded sad, tortured even. I could tell he regretted what he did. I think a part of me even knew he was sorry for his actions. There was no doubt in my mind that he would have done things differently given the chance again. His remorseful demeanor left me vulnerable. Hearing his voice was becoming unbearable. I hated even being on the phone with the man.

When he did call, my heart ached. It's how I knew I'd never get over him. No matter how long it had been, I still missed his touch, his face, and most importantly the way he loved me. At the end of every call he still said it, and I'd even catch myself saying it back. It was habit; one I didn't even consider wrong. I'd made it clear I'd always feel that way about him. For me, I think he was the one true love of my life. Sure, I could have other meaningful relationships, but they'd never be what we had together. They'd never filled the void I had when I thought back to what tore us apart.

Grayson was still trying to win me back. He'd sent flowers, tickets to concerts, and even invited me over for dinner. I always declined on account of being so busy with work. I wasn't lying about it. I was swamped. Being the CEO of Leviathan Agency was hard work. Chad had been right about it consuming my time.

I guess that's why our situation worked for us. We were always around each other, so when it came time for a break we didn't have to look far for a companion. Though we did our best to hide our secret affair, I knew several co-workers were catching on something was happening between us. At first it bothered me. I'd always been happy to talk about my marriage and my wonderful husband. The idea of admitting it had failed broke my heart. When people asked about Grayson I'd simply reply he was fine, as if we were still happily together. I couldn't bring myself to shed light on the truth; we were separated and headed for divorce.

I looked out the glass windows of my office at the full office of employees. Twenty had returned to their old positions. The rest decided to move on to something new. The transition was going successfully without any huge hiccups. For the most part, Chad managed the new entity, while my whole focus was on the agency. Weekly we'd have a meeting with the managers, but aside from that we had different jobs with different companies.

I think it helped us get along. Chad wanted nothing to do with the agency, and because I could run it with my eyes closed, it was never necessary to involve him with concerns.

Charles hadn't been in the office in two weeks. I missed seeing his old butt walking around and stealing candy from people's desks. He'd been known to stand around and talk until he emptied some co-workers jars. I think they got a kick out of it, because almost everyone had something out on display.

Chad told me they were planning on throwing a big

shindig, but I hadn't received the details yet. When I got the mail delivery for the day I saw a fancy envelope I knew was an invitation, so I opened it first. Imagine my surprise when I found it wasn't the invitation for Charles' party, but one for a couples retreat with Grayson. I read over it five times, noticing it was located in the Poconos of Pennsylvania. He'd gone above and beyond on this attempt. Grayson and I had spent our honeymoon in the Poconos. He wanted to take us back to that special place to try to reconnect. The problem was, I didn't know if I wanted to get back what we had.

Don't get me wrong, I loved being married. Grayson was a good husband, up until he slept with Kyla. Since I'd been seeing Chad I kept myself preoccupied, but sometimes at night, as I lay next to him, I wished Grayson was the person beside me. I missed him.

For the rest of the day I kept the invitation out of my mind. It wasn't until I went back to Chad's apartment when I began thinking about it again.

Chad had ordered us Chinese. We sat at the kitchen island eating out of the boxes. "How was your day?" He asked in between chews.

"Busy. I got an invitation for a couples retreat from Grayson."

His brows raised. "Wow. Did you respond?"

"No. Why would I?" I wanted to know why Chad would even ask.

"Because he's still your husband and you have residual feelings for him. Maybe some time together would help you make your mind up."

"My mind up? I thought I already had."

"It's not how I see it. Rach, you're still in love with him."

I don't know why talking about this made me uncomfortable. Chad was always open with me. We were friends, yet I felt like it was something more; something stronger. "He was my husband. Of course I have feelings for him."

"It's more than that, and in case you've forgotten, you're   still   married."
"On paper."

"Legally," he added.

"So, you think I should have a weekend away with him? What good would it do?"

He sat his box down and used a napkin to wipe his lips. "It will either give you closure, or a second chance to make it work. Being in limbo isn't anyway to live your life. You and I both know you haven't seen a divorce lawyer. There's a reason for that."

I wanted to ask him about us. I wanted to talk about how I'd felt while staying with him for almost a month. I wanted to talk to him about our relationship, because there obvious was something happening between us, but Chad acted oblivious. "I think you're wrong. I don't want to be alone with Grayson."

"It's a couple days out of your life. What can it hurt?"

He had a point. If I didn't want Grayson it would be

closure. If my heart was still torn at least I'd stop wondering. I think the biggest hurdle for me was the fact that Chad didn't seem annoyed. He was pushing me to go, which made me feel like I meant nothing to him. To test out the theory, I decided to go ahead and give Grayson a couple days. I didn't have to be intimate to spend time with him. It was just a weekend. "Fine. I'll tell him I'll go."

"I think you'll figure out what you want to do, Rach. Don't you want to make a final decision?"

I shrugged. "I suppose it's time."

Chad agreed and headed into the bedroom to shower, leaving me alone with the rest of my food. I waited until I heard him go into the bathroom to pull out my phone and message Grayson. I don't know why I felt so torn, but I knew I was about to figure it out.

Chapter 26

GRAYSON

Going a month without seeing my wife was something I never thought would happen. I could remember missing her after only a couple days. Now, the inevitable was staring me in the face. She might never come back to me.

Two weeks after Rachel left me I started seeing a psychiatrist. I chose a female doctor, because to some degree I needed to have a woman's perspective. I wanted to know it was possible for a female to sympathize with my situation.

After two sessions she suggested I invite my wife to go on a couples retreat. I was skeptical, especially since Rachel hadn't wanted to be in the same room with me. I couldn't imagine her agreeing to see me for a longer period of time.

That's when I decided I needed to ask her in person. I got in my car and drove to her office, adamant on making her see how important it was for us.

I never expected to run into someone I recognized from being with her the night we split up. As soon as I saw him my heart began to race. Anger filled a void that had been replaced with despair for too long. I'd never wanted to haul off and hit a guy like I did him.

At first glance he acted as if he'd never seen me before. "Can I help you with something, sir?"

"I'm looking for my wife," I said with a smirk. "Rachel. Have you seen her?"

His eyes lit up, and finally he recognized where he'd seen me before. I kept my fists tight until he responded. "She's actually out for a lunch meeting with a client. Did you want me to leave her a message?"

"No!" I quickly replied. "I'd like to wait for her to return. Just point me to her new office."

He raised a brow and took a deep breath. "Look, buddy, I don't think this is a good place for you two to talk. We like to keep it calm here."

"Unless you want my fist in your mouth, you'll guide me to her office." I lowered my voice when someone walked by us. "You think I don't know who you are? I remember you. You're the guy she's been fucking."

He fastened his hand on my arm and led me to a hallway. "Listen, man, don't make this ugly. Rachel isn't here. You and I both know she won't want to come back from a meeting and be faced with whatever you're here to talk to her about. If you want to meet up later I'd be glad to help you set it up. I'm not the enemy."

"Really?" I was amused. "You're screwing my wife."

"Did she tell you that?"

"Not in so many words."

He led me into an office. Right away I could tell it

was his. Pictures of him and the owner, Charles were on a bookcase behind the desk. He took a seat and offered me the one across from him. "Rachel is important to this company. My grandfather cares a lot about her. With that being said, yes, we've become close in the past month. She and I have to work together. We're transitioning into separate entities, and without her a lot of people would have lost their jobs. She's an amazing woman."

"You don't have to tell me. That's why I married her."

He folded his hands together and then released them, only to do it again. I could tell he was thinking. "Why are you here, Grayson?"

"Oh, you want to be on a first name basis?"

"I'm Chad, and like I told you before, I'm not a threat to you. Rachel is goal oriented. I've listened to her cry, yes. I've been there for her, yes. Do I want to steal your wife away, well no. Despite the fact that I'd love to have a relationship with her, I know her heart is still elsewhere."

"Coming here was a mistake." He'd admitted more than I wanted to know. He obviously cared about Rachel. She needed that kind of attention, especially after I'd hurt her. Maybe it was time to give up. She'd clearly moved on.

"Wait," he announced when I stood and turned to leave. "I might not think you waiting for Rachel is a good idea, but you seem like you're desperate to talk to her. To prove I'm not a bad guy, I'll relay whatever you want to be said. If you want to stick around here and wait, I can't stop you."

I pulled out the envelope I'd put the invitation in. I'd made a promise to myself that I'd try my hardest to reach her. I couldn't back down, even if I felt it was a lost cause. "I came here to give her this. It's an invitation to a couples retreat. Our marriage might be over. For all I know it's what you're hoping for. It would be decent of you to let her decided for herself. You say her heart is still with me. I need to know if there's hope. I'm giving this to you in hopes that you'll pass it along. If I were in your shoes I probably wouldn't. You make the call. I think we both need to know where Rachel stands. This will settle it. She'll either reconnect with me, or she'll make sure I know we're through."

He nodded and took the envelope. "Okay. I'll make sure she gets it."

I proceeded to walk out of the office. "For what it's worth, I know you couldn't help yourself. I couldn't either when I met her. She's the whole damn package. I just wish I didn't take her for granted." I waved as I walked out of the office, but didn't turn back. I didn't care what he was thinking about, or prepared to say next. It was killing me, looking at him, picturing him touching her, holding her, and taking away the pain I'd caused.

All I could do was wait to hear from Rachel. If the guy Chad was a good man, he'd let her make up her own mind. Either way I doubted I'd hear from her. I feared my time with Rachel was over a while ago.

Chapter 27

"I can't believe I agreed to this," I said to Chad as we were going down the stairs to the parking garage. Friday had come too fast, and within hours I'd be on my way to spend a weekend with my husband, Grayson, who I hadn't even begun to forgive for destroying our marriage. He may have been trying to convince me otherwise, but I still resented him for cheating, and didn't feel he was wholeheartedly sorry. Sure, he regretted the decision, but six months was a long time to continue something you knew was a bad idea, unless it was important. I couldn't stop thinking about the times he'd come home whistling or beside himself with happiness. I wondered if one of those times he'd been with her, or perhaps all of them. The idea gave me a stomach ache. On few occasions, I'd gotten so upset I'd become sick over it. Yet, here I was, making the choice to spend a couple days with him.

I'd wanted to back out, especially after noticing the way Chad had withdrawn since our talk about it. I felt like every attempt I made to move forward, he was throwing my past into my face, telling me I needed to figure out my life. Maybe he was frustrated being in limbo. We'd been sleeping together for weeks, yet never discussed a future. I wondered what I meant to him on a daily basis, but he made me so happy I didn't want to chance finding out I didn't mean the same to him. I was falling hard for Chad, finding happiness when I was surrounded by pain. He'd saved me in some ways, showing me I was worth fighting for, although in this situation, he'd been the opposite. It was as if he was on Grayson's side. It drove me mad, especially since he'd been around from day one to see the agony I'd gone through.

He'd seen me at my lowest, and brought me back from wanting to give up. Sure, our relationship had been based on sex, but we'd grown into something else, something I wasn't sure how to explain. Chad not begging me to stay home with him was torturing me.

It hurt my feelings, especially since we spent so much of our lives together now. I couldn't recall one single day where we hadn't been together. He made me smile. He taught me how to love my body. He seemed to love it too.

"It's a couple days. It's not like you're being forced. Don't make it harder on yourself."

Arguing was my only way to get my point across. "I haven't wanted to be near the man. Why do you think this could be a good idea?"

He turned and stared me in the eyes. "Do you still love Grayson, Rach?" I used to get offended when he called me that, but now I appreciated having a nickname, especially from Chad.

I shrugged. "I promised to love him forever when we married, but that was destroyed the moment he screwed my daughter's childhood friend. It makes me sick.

I'm torn on how I feel. He broke my heart. It's still breaking."

"A heart can't be broken unless it loves."

He had a valid point. If I didn't love Grayson, I wouldn't have cared who he was screwing. "What about us?" I blurted out.

"Us?" He shook his head and cackled. "We're friends, Rach. You know that. We have a good time together. We're very compatible, so it's fun being together."

"We're more, at least to me we are."

"Nevertheless, you're in love with your husband, who you promised to love forever. Correct? Isn't that what this is about? Grayson wants you back. He's made it abundantly clear. You say he isn't trying, but he is. He's going above and beyond to get you back."

I hated when he had a point. "I suppose."

He lifted his hand up to graze my cheek. "We'll talk when you get back. Until then, I think it's important you focus on this weekend. Give it a chance. Don't leave any rock unturned."

I nodded, even though I didn't agree. I wanted to spend my weekend tangled up in Chad's sheets, where he'd make all my stress dissipate. "I'll miss you," I managed to say.

"Yeah. It's going to be quiet without you around. I'm sure I'll find something to get into. There's a men's physique competition a few of my friends are competing in. I may go check that out."

"Can I call you?" I don't know why, but I felt like this was goodbye, and I hated it.

"I'd rather you not. Don't give Grayson a reason to become angry. Devote your time to him, even if it's to tell him goodbye. You both deserve it. Closure is a bitch, but you can't leave it unresolved."

I hugged Chad, unable to give up hope that I'd come home to him. "Thank you for understanding. You're very kind. I'm lucky to have you in my life. I'm just sorry you have to deal with it, with all of my drama."

"Yeah, I knew what I was getting into. It's cool. I'm not a relationship kind of guy, but I get it. You however, you deserve to be madly in love with a man who wants the same. It's obvious Grayson is trying. Otherwise, he would have given up sooner. You always said he was a good guy, Rach. Maybe this weekend will settle your mind. Maybe you'll say goodbye. Maybe you'll rekindle what you once had for each other."

Tears were forming in my eyes. It was like Chad already knew who I'd want to be with in the long run, so he was letting me go. I wanted him to fight for me, for what was happening between us, but he wouldn't budge. Chad seemed like he couldn't care less about me going to be alone with Grayson, almost as if he expected me to fall back in love with him. It hurt me, because for the past month I'd spent every waking second imagining a life with him. Now I didn't know where my heart would take me, and that scared the shit out of me.

I fastened my hand around his tie and pulled him close to me, my lips dragging over his as I spoke. "Give me a reason to stay. Tell me not to go. Tell me you want me for yourself."

"We don't have time to get into this. You need to leave from here. He's already waiting for you."

I kissed him once again, this time with enough intent to make him reconsider. "I'm sure we can be quick. Don't you want me?"

"Rach, you're playing with fire. This will only complicate things."

I shoved him hard against the cement walls of the stairwell. "Don't make me beg, Chad." I slipped my blazer off, tossing it onto the hard stone floor beneath me. My hands went for his trousers, determined to unbutton them. He pulled me closer, flicking his tongue on my bottom lip before taking my mouth for a lustful ride. We were too engulfed to consider being discovered. I wouldn't have cared. Chad was going to take me in the stairwell, and I was prepared to let him. "Don't stop," I begged.

I freed his erection, keeping one hand firm around his girth. He picked me up, spinning us around until my back was pressed against the wall. My skirt was shoved higher, and my panties off to the side, exposing my pussy. "Is this what you want? You want to be a bad girl?"

I nodded and teased his tongue with mine. "I want to fuck, right here, right now."

He entered me, forcing his way inside my tight walls. My hold weakened as the engulfment of sensations rushed over me. I bellowed out his name as he forcefully thrust. "Don't stop."

"Your pussy's soaked, Rach. I'm going to come fast."

I wanted him to. I wanted to feel him tightening and losing control. It's how I wanted to think about him when I was away. I needed to know he wasn't going to go out and replace me, because without him I'd be lost and overwhelmed with remorse. Chad took the pain away, again and again.

"Harder. Slam into me. Show me how you like it, Chad. Show me how you come."

He lost it. Those few words helped it happen quick. He let his hold relax and I felt my feet hitting the ground. His heavy breathing was tucked against my neck. He kissed me there, slowly, using a little tongue. "Damn, woman. Just damn."

He backed away from me, breaking our connection, his pants around his ankles. "What?" I asked.

"I know what you're doing."

He couldn't, but even if it was possible, I refused to argue. I was too elated. "Deal with it. When I get back to my apartment Sunday, I want you there."

"Rach, don't make plans with me yet. You don't know what will happen."

"I do. I already know."

He brought his finger up to my lips to stop me from speaking then shook his head. "If only life were that easy." He paused for a moment. "I want you to have a nice weekend. Wherever your heart leads you know I've enjoyed being close to you, getting to know the person you are on the inside, and without clothes. Life is crazy. Shit happens we can't control. We have to live it to the fullest." His hand came up and brushed my cheek. I leaned into it and closed my eyes. "Be safe driving. I'll see you on Monday."

I watched Chad walk away from me. He went so fast I knew I wouldn't be able to catch up in heels. There was so much I wanted to say to him, to know about how he felt, but I didn't have time to ask him. Maybe he was right. Maybe I needed to find closure before I looked toward the future.

Chapter 28

We had plans to meet at a park and ride off the beltway, in between her office and our home. I'd been sitting there waiting for nearly fifteen minutes when she finally pulled into the spot next to me.

Rachel had never looked better. She'd changed her appearance, and even began wearing more makeup. She seemed less stressed, up until her eyes locked on mine. Then I watched a concerned grimace take over her face. I got out of the car to greet her and place her bag in the trunk. She rolled her eyes and met me a the rear of the vehicle. "You look nice," I noted.

"Whatever. Don't think that charming me will change the way I feel. I'm doing this for closure, Grayson. I'm tired of being in limbo."

"Fair enough. Although, I would appreciate it if we left our baggage here in this parking lot, and I'm not talking about your overnight bag. It's only fair if we go into this with open minds, Rachel. I'm not asking you to relive the past. I'm asking for a new future, where we could start over and build something stronger than we've ever had before."

"I understand what you're asking of me. I'll do my best. This isn't exactly how I would have liked this to go, but I'm here and I'll try to keep an open mind."

"What about the guy you're seeing? Chad?"

"You know who he is?" I finally got her attention. "When did you figure it out?"

"It doesn't matter. I need to know this weekend will be about us. It's only fair to leave everything else in our lives behind. It's for three days. That's all I'm asking. If you decide we're over, I'll watch you walk away. I won't fight with you. It's ultimately your decision."

Rachel tossed her bag in the trunk and headed for the passenger seat of the car without replying to my comment. I couldn't tell whether she was annoyed, or afraid of what I knew. It didn't matter. Unless I had her full attention this weekend wouldn't help us.

I'd been driving for ten miles before she spoke. "Are we going to stop somewhere for dinner? I'm starving."

"I had a place in mind. It's about twenty minutes from here. Can you wait that long?"

She stared out the window as she answered. "Yeah."

The place I wanted to take her was special. I knew she wouldn't remember it until we arrived. We hadn't gone there since my first wife had passed away. It was on the way to the institution she'd been living at. We'd taken the drive to pick up the little bit of her belongings she'd been able to keep. On the way home we were hungry and exhausted. We pulled over at the first place we came to, which happened to be a motel with a small diner attached. After we had a home-cooked meal, we sat there talking for hours, finally succumbing to our fatigued bodies. We got a room, but after an emotional embrace, one thing led to another. We stayed up half the night making love, discovering new things about each other, and setting the pace for a future wedding. That following weekend I asked her to be my wife. We'd never looked back after that trip, and I hoped somewhere in her heart she'd be able to reconnect with me again.

Fortunate for me, this wasn't the only surprise I had up my sleeve. Like it or not, we weren't going to a couples retreat, not like one she assumed. I'd made reservations for a cabin, secluded from everything else. We'd be in the middle of the woods with no cell service or electricity. It was a desperate attempt, but I knew once I got her there she'd have no choice but to give me a chance. I wasn't thinking she'd go along with it calmly. I was hoping for a miracle to guide us in the right direction for our future. I already knew where I wanted to be in in five years time. It was up to Rachel to make her own decision, whether it was with me, or someone else.

It wasn't long before I pulled into the old motel parking lot. Rachel hadn't been paying much attention until the gravel started picking up as the tires moved further. She took in her surroundings, finally turning to address the situation. "I know this place."

"I was hoping you would. This is our first stop." She unbuckled her seat belt. "It's not going to end the same as last time, I can assure you of that."

I nodded, but kept my opinions to myself. She didn't need to see me get upset. I wouldn't let her feeling sorry for me allow her to make decisions she'd regret later.

We entered in the establishment and were quickly seated across from each other. Rachel held the menu up to keep me from seeing her face. "Do you remember what we had last time?"

"It was ten years ago, Grayson. Give me a break."

"You had their signature sandwich. It's called a Rachel. It's turkey, swiss and coleslaw on a bun. You said it was the best sandwich you'd ever eaten."

She lowered the menu and squinted her eyes. "That was easy to answer. Once you saw it you remembered."

I accepted it could have been the case, but it wasn't true. She went on and on about a food having her name. "Whatever. So, is that what you're ordering?"

"I'm not sure yet."

I kept staring down at my menu, too focused on Rachel to concentrate enough to read.

The waitress came to take our orders and Rachel went first. She ordered the same sandwich and then began to tell the waitress what I was having. "I'll have the Rachel, light thousand island on the side please. He's going to have the pulled pork, with the Carolina style sauce, and the hand cut fries. We'll both have a sweet tea, one with lemon and one without."

I was impressed. As soon as the waitress walked away I saw her peering into my eyes. "Two can play this game, Grayson. You're easy to guess. You always have the same things."

"I think it's a little more than being perspective. I think you remember the details from the last time we were here, back when we were insanely in love with each other."

"Thinking about back then makes my heart hurt." She looked at the menu again. "I wish this place served wine."

"They may not serve it, but I bought a few bottles of your favorite to take with us."

She sort of smiled. "That was kind of you."

"I'm trying, Rachel. I really am."

"Noted and appreciated."

"How was your day at work?" I figured small talk would help pass the time.

She shrugged. "Work is overwhelming at the moment. I have a lot riding on my shoulders. When I took on the new position I was under the impression that I'd have a little leeway as far as delegating jobs to other people. So far it hasn't happened."

I didn't want to ask about her friend, because I knew the topic of him had to stay off limits. "So you're doing too much?"

"Some days I feel like I am. Everything falls on me. If there is a problem with anything agency related I have to deal with it. Maybe if I wasn't under so much stress already I could handle it better. Right now it's impossible."

"I'm sorry for my part in that, babe. I know it's been rough for you."

"I'm not here to listen to your apologies. I think we've both said enough. Maybe you're right. Maybe this weekend we both need to get away from reality and focus on what's important."

"I'm glad you feel that way."

"I'm not making you promises, Grayson. I can't."

"I get it. As long as we're together this weekend, it's enough for me."

With that being said we enjoyed our lunches, almost like it was old times. When we got back on the road I was hopeful. Rachel seemed to have relaxed, and I prayed she'd remain comfortable when she found out where we would be staying, and why I'd gone to extremes to have her to myself.

Chapter 29

RACHEL

We'd been driving for what felt like hours, probably because I was uncomfortable being this close to him. I hated knowing at any moment he could reach over and touch me. The idea of it still made my skin crawl. What made matters worse was knowing what I'd done with Chad only hours before. His touch was still familiar in my mind, and parts of my skin smelled like his cologne. I closed my eyes and focused on our last moments together. Chad's fingers traced my lips, giving me chills throughout my body. I recalled the anticipation of his touch elsewhere, but right as I began to replay it in my mind I heard Grayson speaking. "Did you hear me, Rachel?"

"No, sorry. I must have been somewhere else for a second."

"Did you need to stop and get anything before head up to where we'll be staying?"

"I'm good. I'm sure they'll have anything we might need."

He pulled over at a local grocery and told me he'd be back. I sat there for a few seconds, finally giving in to my own needs and pulled out my phone. I sent Chad a message. I wanted him to know I was thinking of him already.

Wishing I was there with you. – R

He replied immediately.

You are supposed to be focused on your husband. – C

I can't help it. The stairwell didn't leave me with enough. I want more. – R

Don't tease me, Rach. I'll see you Monday. Try to have a nice time. You're getting away from work too. Enjoy it. – C

What if I can't? What if I already know where I need to be? – R

I'll be here when you get back. Promise me you'll put all your efforts into this weekend. It will do you good. You need this. – C

I'll text when I can. – R

Rachel, don't. Pretend I don't exist this weekend. Being with me is clouding your judgment. You need to focus on your future, and how much Grayson will be apart of it. – C

He's coming. I need to go. Miss you. – R

I turned off my device and tucked it back in my purse right before Grayson climbed in the car with three bags of groceries.

I was confused. "Why would we need all that? Doesn't the retreat provide meals?"

He wouldn't respond. "Grayson, seriously, what's going on?"

"It's just a couple more minutes up the road, Rachel. Let me get us there before you start complaining."

I was already regretting this weekend. It was possible he was driving me to a secluded location to decapitate me for seeking revenge with another man, and falling for him. Maybe I deserved to meet my demise by his hands. Maybe this was how our story ended.

We turned and started driving up a mountain. The road was gravel and dirt, and there wasn't a house or electrical line the whole way. We saw a few deer crossing and running through thickets. I watched the beams of light coming down through the trees, guiding us up the rough terrain. Finally we came to a stop in front of an old wooden cabin. It had a small porch on the front and two rocking chairs. I turned to look at Grayson and then back at the tiny cottage. "This is where we're staying?"

"Don't hate it yet. It's going to be fun."

"Where are the other cabins? Isn't the retreat with other couples?"

"Rachel, it's just us. I didn't want distractions or other people's opinions. This is between you and me. We can figure this out together. Just give it a try."

I couldn't seem to find compassion for Grayson, especially in this case. I wasn't against camping when Stephanie was younger, but this wasn't necessary. I needed amenities.

"This is a terrible idea."

Grayson ignored me and began carrying the bags of groceries onto the porch. I fetched my clothes from the trunk and followed behind him, eager to see what was awaiting inside.

Unlike the worn outer shell, the inside had been kept up. Two leather couches faced one another, leading to a beautiful stone fireplace. The kitchen was in the back of the cabin, and it was open to a small table with four chairs. Steps were on the far side of the structure, leading to what I assumed were two bedrooms.

I let out a sigh and searched for light switches to better assess the area. "Please tell me there's electric."

He chuckled. "Nope. We have to fend for ourselves. We're going colonial style this weekend."

"If you expect me to make some clothes and churn butter you've got another thing coming," I noted.

He laughed at me. "If you start doing that I'll worry about your sanity."

I had to smile. For a brief moment I forgot why we were there. My laughter seemed to be contagious as we stood there in the room together.

I helped Grayson get everything carried in, and actually started to appreciate being away from the hustle and bustle of life and work. Maybe I needed this break, perhaps we both did.

Grayson told me to check out the back deck while he put the groceries away and took our bags to our rooms. I half expected him to stick our things in the same one, but kept my mouth shut until I could find out if it was true.

A few moments later, I heard the slider opening. Grayson was carrying two glasses of wine. I sat up and took one out of his hand before he was able to sit down beside me. "It's beautiful isn't it?"

"It is." Birds were flying around, and the trees were blowing in the breeze. The leaves were starting to change to gorgeous fall hues, and it smelled so fresh, like earth and nature. The sun would be setting shortly, and I knew it would be a spectacular view. Aside from the normal sounds, it was extremely quiet. We couldn't hear cars or trucks. We hadn't passed a single dwelling for the whole adventure up the mountain. "Where is the closest neighbor?"

"I have no clue. I'm pretty sure it's just us for a good distance. Why?" He questioned. "Are you planning on running away."

I smirked and gave him a quick glance. "It depends on your intentions."

"My intentions are from the heart, I assure you."

"Then I suppose I can stick around." I sipped at my favorite wine, appreciating the little details he was taking to make me comfortable. "So what's on the agenda this evening?"

"Nothing. We can relax and have a nice dinner later. I'm making you Salmon in a sweet pepper coating on the grill, accompanied by fresh asparagus and baked potatoes."

"Sounds great. I haven't had that in a while." I knew

what he was doing. Grayson was prepared to shower me with everything he knew I favored. He was determined to impress me. "I would have been fine with anything."

"Only the best for you, Rachel. It's always been that way. I hope you know that."

What he was saying was true. Grayson had always gone above and beyond to make me happy. This wasn't him attempting to push his way back into my heart. He'd been generous since the day I met him. It was the reason I fell so deeply in love with him in the first place.

"I know you're going to want to talk. It's probably best if you give the wine some time. I tend to be brutally honest after I drink, so you'll get the answers you've been waiting for."

"Or the ones I can't bear to handle."

I sipped at my glass again. "It's possible."

"I love you, Rachel. It's only ever been you. Even when Molly and I were married, I never felt a connection like we have. I know you don't believe it, but —"

"I do. I know how you feel about me. I understand how hard this has been, not just for me but you as well. I can see the toll it's taken on you. You look tired. I went through a time where I couldn't close my eyes without it hurting. I stayed awake, dwelling on the situation instead of letting my body rest. If you're going through it, I can understand how difficult it's been."

"It has. I wake up and you're not there next to me. I keep thinking it's all a bad dream, but I know better. I have to relive every moment I spent ruining our commitment. I can't hate you. I don't. If the roles were reversed I would have probably done the same thing. I wouldn't have wanted to be alone."

I wasn't ready to get into this with him. "If the roles were reversed it wouldn't have happened to begin with."

"You mean to tell me if that young buck threw himself at you you'd be able to restrain?"

I looked away while thinking about Chad. The idea of him coming onto me. The memories of how it felt when he touched me that first time. The sound of his voice when he whispered my name. I had to close my eyes. My heart was beginning to beat faster, and I was losing track of the purpose of the conversation. "We'll never truly know will we? What's done is done. Neither one of us can take back what we've done. Maybe in some ways we both committed adultery."

"Yeah, but I set it all into motion. I take full blame." I could hear his voice cracking. I leaned over and refilled my glass, trying to avoid my own emotional carnage.

He continued. "Rachel, I don't know how to go on without you. I couldn't do a real couples retreat because I can't be anywhere without losing my shit. I've made a terrible mistake. I've destroyed what we had, and I already know there's no hope to get it back."

It was impossible to hold in the tears. We'd been alone like this once before, and it ended with him holding me while I slept. It didn't matter where I was in life, Grayson's arms would always represent comfort for me. His mistake was like a whirlwind of destruction, but at the end of the day we had ourselves to blame for getting to where we were now. I'd struggled, day after day feeling betrayed and lost. I'd gone through the emotions of losing the man I loved, to falling hard for another. Now, being this close to Grayson again, I wondered if I was really where I wanted to be, or was I running from the only life I've ever wanted.

Perhaps Chad was right. Maybe I did need to spend time with Grayson. It was possible this would change everything. Until I knew what I wanted for sure, I was prepared to do whatever it took to figure it out.

Chapter 30

Imagine being so close you could touch the one you loved, but not being able to reach those few inches to do so. That's how I felt sitting next to Rachel and hearing her weep. Her sobs were inflicted by my actions. Once again I was pulling at her heartstrings, and I didn't know what to say or do to make her feel better. I didn't even know if I was the person she needed to make it go away.

After a while I knew it was useless to stick around. I got up and began to prepare dinner. There were a few times where I had to stop and take a few deep breaths to relax. It was hard imagining her forgiving me. I knew it when I asked her to come. With time running out, I needed to figure out a way to break through her barrier. She had to let me in again, or else this would all have been for nothing.

Rachel came inside a little later, carrying an empty bottle of wine. Minus the one glass I'd had, she'd drank the entire thing. Since I knew better than anyone how much of a lightweight she was, I wondered how I was going to open the doors of communication with her three sheets to the wind. "Are you okay?"

"I will be when you open another bottle."

"What if we wait until dinner is served? I don't want you passing out on me before the main course."

She shrugged. "Whatever. Do you need help?"

I handed her two plates and some silverware. "Just set us up. I'll bring everything over to the table."

She walked over and set two places, sitting down at one. She was different, but still as beautiful as ever. Her hair was styled in wavy curls, and I'd never seen her have so much color in it before. Then there were her nails. They were a dark red. She'd never painted them a color, but always gone for a nude French style. The woman sitting before me had changed, yet she was the one I vowed to love forever. I'd broken promises, but my love hadn't faltered. Still, I didn't think it was enough to get her back.

The only problem with not having electricity was fixing everything on the outside grill. I'd prepped the food in the kitchen, and taken it outside to cook. After several trips, the food was ready to eat.

Dinner was finally served, and once we were sitting across from one another I felt anxious again. Rachel began cutting up her fish, while I focused on filling her glass and keeping her content. I'd opened the doors to the back porch and a light breeze was blowing in. The candles lit so we were able to see made for a good ambiance. "I'll probably light a fire after dinner. It might get chilly."

"Let me guess, it's the only source of heat."

"You'd be right," I said while aiming my fork toward her. "It adds a bit of tranquility, don't you think?"

"I think you're planning on getting me on that rug over there. It's not going to happen."

I bit my tongue to keep from saying something that could offend her. "You know me better than that, Rachel. I'd never push."

She raised her brow. "Really? So how was it that you got Kyla to sleep with you? What did you promise her? Did you buy her extravagant gifts? Did you promise her stability?"

"No. It's not like that at all." I shook my head and placed my fork down on my plate. "I told you before, I never came onto Kyla, not even once. She came after me. She basically threw herself at me. I know you don't believe it, but it's true. Not one time did I ever think about her in any other way aside from being Steph's friend. I never asked for this to happen. I know it did, and I can't turn back time, but I'm begging you to let it go. She means nothing to me. She never did. I fucked her, just like you fucked your friend. You say it's not the same, but isn't it? You waited how many days to turn to someone else?"

She opened her mouth to speak, but closed it without saying anything.

"Don't forget I saw you through the window, Rachel. It doesn't matter if you were acting out or seeking revenge. You fucked someone else, and I'm pretty sure you still are. You think it doesn't rip me to shreds?"

"I know it does," she argued. "I know I've hurt you. You still cheated though."

"Rachel, we're still married. Telling me you want a divorce doesn't make it legal. You are still my wife. We've gone longer without being together before. This isn't irreparable. You know it isn't. Stop running away from me. I need you, and I think you need me to."

"You're wrong."

"About what part?"

"About me needing you. I've done fine since we've parted ways, Grayson. In fact, I've never been happier. You want to pull Chad into the conversation, let me just tell you how amazing he's been. He's always there for me. He has my back, even when it comes to forgiving you. He told me to come on this trip. Could you be that unselfish? Would you be willing to let me go for someone else?"

"I can't compete." I shook my head. It was obvious she wasn't going to give in. It was always her way or none at all. "No matter what I say to you, you've made your mind up already."

I couldn't control my emotions. Instead of finishing my food, I stood and threw my napkin on my plate, then walked outside, where I let go, not caring if she could hear me or not.

Chapter 31

I never should have opened my mouth. I'd gone and broken his heart again. Bringing Chad into our conversation was a huge mistake. Grayson would never be able to look past it when I kept throwing it in his face.

I missed Chad. If I were at a cabin in the woods with him we'd spend it in each other's arms. However, knowing I was this close to Grayson, the declared love of my life, I wondered if this wasn't right where I was supposed to be.

I took a couple bites of the food he'd prepared just for me. My teeth were chattering, and if I listened closely I could hear him bellowing out his pain on the porch. I sat there for a couple seconds thinking about what he'd been through. Was he right? Was I doing the same thing to him? If so, how could I have been so insensitive? How could I have let myself fall for someone else when the one person I needed to love me was waiting for me to come back to him?

I hated myself.

Before I could reconsider, I left my plate on the table and rushed outside. He turned when he heard footsteps. The remorse shown across his face made me sick to my stomach. I wondered if he was picturing me with Chad, feeling the same sort of disgust.

I reached out and touched his arm. "Grayson, I'm sorry. I wanted you to suffer. I felt like it helped me cope."

He shook his head. "It's killing me. Being here with you was a mistake. I can't do this. I know you're done, so if you want to go home we'll pack up tonight. I can't force you to love me. I can't force you to choose me when it's clear you'll never forgive me for what I did to us."

"I did it to," I said in a whisper. "We both broke our vows. You were right. I'm a hypocrite."

"You did what you felt necessary at the time. I don't blame you for being happy, Rachel. I wish it was that easy for me. I wish there was someone else on this earth to take the pain away, but I know no one will ever compare to you. Maybe I took you for granted. Maybe I didn't value your needs."

"You did," I softly replied. "You were always wonderful to me. I think that's why it hurts so much. I never expected you to do that to me. I never thought you'd stray."

I was trembling, my hands shaking so much I put them in my pockets. I tried to turn away, but as the tears poured from my eyes I knew I couldn't hide the way I was feeling. Grayson knew me. He was experiencing the same emotions. "I love you so much, Rachel."

It was time to stop fighting. I'd buried my feelings for too long. "I love you too."

He sniffled and wiped his face with his hands. "I'll clean up dinner and load the car."

I waited for him to walk by me before responding.

"Wait!" he turned to face me. "I think we should stay, at least for tonight."

"You do?" He seemed shocked.

I motioned with my head. "I've positive." I held out my hand for him to take. "Let's build a fire and finish our dinner in front of it. We don't have to talk. Maybe it's better if we say nothing at all. At this point, we need to stop fighting. I'm tired of bickering with no resolution. Either way this ends, I want us to be friends, Grayson. I need you in my life. I know I said I didn't, but I was angry. I married you because you were my best friend. I miss us."

He pulled me into his arms, offering nothing but a firm hug. "I miss you too."

It was all it took for me to feel overwhelmed. Grayson was the man I promised to love for the rest of my life. I never doubted it either. He'd been everything to me since we started dating, and as much as I tried to deny it now, he still held a huge part of my heart. That being said, I yearned to find resolution, no matter where was heart was about to take me.

Once the fire was ignited, I sat on the couch watching the flames and feeling the steady warmth resonating from it. Grayson joined me eventually, after insisting on cleaning up dinner. He had to use a gallon of store bought water to do the dishes, so I'm sure it took some finagling. There was a well outside with a hand pump, but he insisted on using the jugs he'd purchased.

At first he sat across from me, silently staring into the flames. I got up and walked over, closing the distance between us by occupying the space next to him. "Is this okay?"

He reached over and touched my hand. When he tightened his grip I didn't pull away. "It's good,"

I rested my head on his shoulder. "It's nice."

"I don't expect to move fast, Rachel. I know it will take us time."

I wasn't sure what he was implying. Did he assume this meant we were getting back together, and if so, what was I to do about my feelings for Chad?

Was it possible to love two men completely differently at the same time?

"Good, because I think I need it."

Grayson was still wearing his wedding ring, where I'd taken mine off weeks before. I'd placed it in my purse after the first day I discovered his affair, and hadn't checked for it since. "I promised you forever, so take your time."

We were silent for a few minutes, both staring into the fire, looking for answers to all our problems. Then Grayson asked me a question, and it would confused the hell out of me. "Do you love him?"

I turned and looked at my estranged husband without an answer. I swallowed a lump in my throat and glanced in another direction, unable to face him when the truth was written across my face.

"Rachel, please. I need to know the truth."

"Why?" My lips were chattering again. "What good

will it do?"

"You're right. It will hurt me, but I think I deserve the truth. Something tells me I already know, but I want to hear it from your lips."

The truth lingered in my brain, while my body was losing control to remain strong. I had to be honest with myself, but the problem was I really didn't know. I cared for Chad. It was obvious. I loved being around him, and spending time alone. He made me smile, and helped me through a lot of tough times, but was it love? Was it enough to choose him over Grayson? Had I already made my mind up before stepping foot in this cabin?

As I struggled for an answer I looked into Grayson's eyes. They were pleading with me to give him the response he deserved. For the first time in months I knew exactly what was right and wrong. I was fully aware, which way I wanted to go, and who I wanted to spend the rest of my life with.

I took a deep breath and finally gave Grayson exactly what he'd been waiting for.

"Yes. I love him, but…" He stood before I could keep him next to me. "Grayson, wait. Please hear me out. I have more to say."

"There's nothing left to discuss. You love another man." He was bawling, and I felt awful.

"It's not like what we have. I appreciate him."

"Yeah, well you sure as hell don't appreciate me."

"That's not true. I know in time we could-."

"We could what? Be friends? Have cookouts where the two of you come over and talk about how you got together? No thanks."

"You're being ridiculous. I'd never expect that to happen." It was understandable he was upset, but I'd never rub my happiness in his face. It was obvious this destroyed him.

"I know he told you to come with me this weekend. Why? Does he want you to commit? Is this what it's about? Did he persuade you so you'd have closure with me? Does he want to move on in and keep you for himself?"

"No! Stop it!" I was desperate to rectify the situation, but couldn't figure out how to erase what I'd said. My feelings for Chad were new, therefore blinding me of what we could be to each other in the future. Chad didn't want a relationship. Whatever I felt we were, wasn't how he saw us. There would be no future.

Grayson offered me stability. If I forgave him we could have a happy life together. He wanted to be married to me; to spend the rest of our lives loving each other.

"The truth is, I think I need to be alone for a while. My feelings for Chad don't compare to what we've shared. He'll never be you, Grayson, but the damage is done. We've screwed up our marriage. We've made this mess between us. You want the truth?"

He flipped his palms as he replied. "I guess I do."

"The truth is, I wish we could go back. I miss our life. I miss knowing you were coming home to me every night. I miss feeling like nothing could ever tear us apart. That's the truth, Grayson. It's all I've ever known. Enough of this who do you love more bullshit. I love you, but we can't keep doing this each other. This has to stop."

Before I knew what was happening, Grayson lunged toward me, pressing his lips against mine. I pulled away, flustered and shocked. Then it hit me. This would be the last time we touched each other. I was telling him we were over, and this was his reaction – a final attempt to be close to me.

I can't explain the connection I immediately felt between us. One minute I was enraged, and the next I was wrapping my arms around him and kissing him back. He picked me up and carried me to the couch, where he sat me down and finally joined me.

Kissing him was easy, comfortable even. I'd practiced doing it so many times I could do it effortlessly. In that moment there were no affairs or conflicts. It was just the two of us, connecting the way we used to.

In those few minutes everything became clear again, except this time I wanted my life back; the one I shared with Grayson.

Before things went too far, Grayson backed away. It gave me time to think about what would happen if we continued. Since I'd been with Chad earlier, I felt it necessary to halt what was happening. "We need to stop," I whispered against his lips.

"Why?"

It broke my heart to tell him. "Trust me. It's best if we take this slow. I promised you the weekend. Let's take our time. Just be here with me. Pretend nothing else exists except for us."

"You were with him today, weren't you?" His accusations made my stomach curl. I could feel my dinner making an unexpected presence. *How could he know me so well?*

"No," I lied.

"Rachel, I know when you're keeping the truth from me." He got up and left the room. I adjusted my shirt and went after him, praying I could calm him down.

"Don't be angry. I didn't want to come. I was in denial. I wasn't ready." "This was a mistake. You keep blaming me, but you're the one who gave up on us. You're the one," he repeated.

I was a sobbing mess. "You're right. It's my fault. I should have given it more time. I shouldn't have allowed myself to fall for another man to hide my true feelings for you. I did it. All of it. Blame me for our marriage ending, Grayson, go ahead. I know it's what you want, so the burden is off of your conscience."

"I never said I was innocent."

I cried into my hands, silently pleading with God to strike me with lightning and end the pain. I couldn't handle it any longer. I wanted it to disappear, no matter how I needed to make it happen. "We can't keep doing this. Trying isn't getting us anywhere. Grayson, you'll always have a piece of my heart, but it's obvious we can't make it work. Too much has happened. We've both made mistakes, and now we have to suffer the repercussions. Just face it, our marriage was over weeks ago, and there's nothing we can do to get it back."

Then it happened. We stood out on the porch holding each other as we broke down. This was our goodbye – the end of something we thought could last forever.

Chapter 32

My plan had backfired. We left the cabin Saturday morning, after staying up all night in separate rooms. I should have known it would end this way, but I couldn't have imagined how unbearable it would feel.

Rachel had moved on. She'd probably be happy with her new beau. He seemed like a nice guy, and they obviously shared similar interests.

As for me, I'd spend the rest of my days alone. There would never be another woman who could give me what she could. I'd never love someone like I love her. No matter how much time would pass, I knew she was it for me.

After I dropped her off at her car, I drove straight to the house. Surprisingly, I pulled into my driveway to find my daughter there. Normally I would have frowned upon visitors after such a shitty night, but I welcomed her friendly smile when I opened the door. "What are you doing home, Dad? I thought you said you rented the place until Sunday."

I frowned. "It didn't work out the way I thought it would."
"What do you mean?" I could tell she was sad by my news. Stephanie loved our family, so the idea of it breaking up permanently was terrible news.

"Your mom and I can't get past what's been done. We both made mistakes, and sometimes they're too involved to forgive."

"What do you mean, both? What did Mom do?"

I felt worse. Obviously Rachel hadn't told Stephanie about her little boy toy. "Sweetie, your mom has been seeing someone. She's moved on." I had to clench my jaw to keep my composure. "Our marriage is over, and there's nothing any of us can do. We made the choice together. I want you to know that. It wasn't easy, but we did it together. It's best for all of us if we get past it and move forward with our lives. No more living without answers."

"How do you know she's with someone else? She never said a thing to me."

"Honestly, I don't know if it's serious. All I do know is that we couldn't connect, not the way we should have been able to."

Stephanie hugged me. I was surprised she was giving me support, considering how angry she'd been over my affair. "I'm sorry, Daddy. I wish there was something I could do."

"Are you staying the night? I could use some company."

She smiled. "I am. I was just about to rent some movies. Are you up for a night of horror flicks?"

"As long as there isn't romance, I'm good."

Stephanie brought up Kyla before I was able to. "I spoke to Kyla the other day. She finally came clean about everything. I know she provoked you. I know she lied to Mom about the affair." She looked down at her hands. "You hurt me when I found out the truth, but I'm actually glad I know. She's not a friend to me. She used me, and I'll blame her for destroying our family."

"It's my fault, Steph. You know it is."

She nodded. "Maybe in some ways. Although, I can tell you've been torn apart over your breakup with Mom. Who knows. Maybe she'll come back to you. Maybe it's not over."

I cupped her chin and tried to smile. "I wish that were the truth, sweetie. I really do. Can you ever forgive me for what I did? Is it too soon?"

She shrugged. "You're my only father. I love you unconditionally. You taught me to forgive. I think it's time we all got a fresh start, don't you?"

I held her close, feeling like as long as I had her in my life I'd be okay. Stephanie would make sure I was never alone. "What would I do without you?" "I don't know, probably starve, or die of malnutrition," she teased.

We played on each other's words until the movie started. I didn't pay any attention to what was going on. All I could think about was Rachel. I wanted to know she was okay, and that she hadn't run right into her lover's arms. I knew we were over, but I still wondered if she regretted the decision. Was Stephanie right? Was there a chance she'd come back to me someday?

I think I'd come to the conclusion that I'd spend

every single day appreciating what I had left in my life. Who knows, maybe one day we could be friends again. That's what I hoped for, because giving up was never going to sit well with my heart.

Chapter 33

I'd left Chad three messages with no response. Since I wasn't in any condition to talk about the previous night, I headed to my apartment instead of his, where I spent the entire afternoon sulking in my own misery. For the life of me, I never expected to hurt so much when it came to saying goodbye to Grayson.

I'd been nauseous ever since climbing in the car with him earlier. Now that I'd arrived at home, it hadn't gotten any better.

It was hard thinking about Chad and then my mind going back to Grayson. I was more confused now than ever, and had it not been for my actions before leaving for the weekend with Grayson, maybe things would have gone differently. There was a chance we would have stayed the whole weekend, reconnecting and finding love again.

I'd destroyed that opportunity. I'd let my relationship with Chad ruin my chances of getting back my happy ever after with Grayson.

By seven p.m. I was starting to feel annoyed. I knew Chad said he would find something to do, but he always kept his phone on him. It made me suspicious, like he was out with another woman. If he was, I couldn't get angry. I didn't even have a right to be jealous. He'd made it abundantly clear we weren't in a committed relationship. No matter how I felt about him, it was quite obvious his perception of our friendship wasn't the same.

I'd made choices I wasn't proud of, and now I wondered if I was even where I wanted to be; sitting all alone in an apartment, instead of in my home with my family.

Feeling sorry for myself was something I'd come to be used to. It seemed like whenever I was sad about something, it was self inflicted. I'd chose to seduce Chad in the parking garage stairwell, knowing I was about to be in the vehicle with Grayson. What kind of idiot would do something so reckless?

This kind.

They say you don't know what you've got until it's gone. My marriage was over. I'd claimed I'd wanted it for a month, but now that it was final, I was beginning to think I'd been wrong.

By ten p.m. I was losing my grip on reality. I hadn't received a single call from Chad, and my mind wouldn't turn off. I'd showered, and cried. Tried to eat, thrown up, and then cried. Then I cried some more. I even attempted to do a little work, and ended up in tears. Slowly I was losing my ability to hold on to anything.

A knock on my door sent me flying toward it. I swung it open, seeing Chad standing on the other side. My arms wrapped around him, like a child lost from their parents. "I had the worst day ever."

He stepped inside and closed the door behind us. "I thought you agreed to stay the whole weekend?"

"I couldn't. He knows about us. He knew we were together yesterday. It's a terrible mess, but it's over. He doesn't want me anymore." Saying it out loud caused me to break down again. Chad distanced himself from my body to be able to look at me.

"What do you mean? He doesn't want you? What happened?"

We sat down close to each other and I began to explain everything that happened, and what we'd discussed. I could tell by the look on his face that he wasn't thrilled his name was brought into it. "I thought you promised to keep an open mind."

"I did. We even connected. We had a moment, and it felt like we were back to our old life, but I had to stop him. He wanted something I wasn't willing to give him."

Right away Chad knew why. "Because you'd been with me earlier, right? That's it. You couldn't live with yourself if you slept with both of us in the same day."

I nodded. "I didn't tell him. He guessed it. After that his mind was made up. We're through, and a part of me feels like it's dead." "Don't cry, Rach. You'll get through this." He cupped my cheeks and forced me to look at him. "You're strong and independent. I know it feels like it's the end of your life, but you're wrong. Maybe it's the beginning of something new instead."

"With you?" I asked.

"It's not the time to discuss this. You've been through a lot. How about you try to relax and get some sleep? I'm sure you'll feel a little better in the morning."

"Will you at least stay with me?"

Chad ran his hand through my hair. "Of course. Come on. Let's get you settled." I don't know why, but I felt like as soon as I closed my eyes he was going to leave. I fought it, unwilling to give up and wake to find him gone.

I'm not real sure how long he'd been there, or what time it was, but I turned to see him looking at his phone. He was typing pretty fast. I new it had to be an email, rather than a text from the amount he was writing. "Is everything okay at the office?"

"Yeah. I'm just making plans for a business trip I'm taking next week."

I sat up. "You didn't tell me you were going anywhere." I corrected my statement. "I mean, you never mentioned it before."

"You've been busy. It's only for a few days. I'm going to California to meet with some potential companies we may sub-contract to. We'll need to rent equipment until our revenue is good enough to make purchases from. I've got a list of people to meet with, and figured it was better to do it in person."

"Chad, where were you today? I called you a lot of times. I left messages."

"I made plans, Rach. Why are you being so weird?"

"Do you love me?"

From the way his face reacted I think I already got my answer. He remained quiet for a moment, probably thinking about how to let me down easily. When he responded I was in shock.

"Yeah, I think I do. No, I know I do. Are you happy now? Can you settle down?"

I tried to smile, finally feeling a bit of happiness despite the pain I'd been experiencing. "Yes, I think so. Thank you for telling me."

"Rachel, love is complicated. You know that more than anyone. As beautiful as it can be, it can also be painful. I told you before I didn't want a relationship. I meant it, but not for the reasons you probably assume. It's not that I don't want you in my life. I just know where I'm headed, you won't be able to come."

"Where you're headed? I don't want your money. I mean, you're powerful. You'll be successful. There's no doubt about it."

"Rach, I'm not staying in D.C. forever. My grandfather knew I'd planned to move to the West Coast as soon as the company was up and running. Most of our clients are there, and we'll need a location centralized to cater to them. I can't be here and expect them to come to me."

"I don't understand. Leviathan is here. It's where the office is located."

"It's where the agency is located," he corrected. "The new company will need to be out in California."

"Why are you just telling me this?"

"Because I knew if I told you you'd push me away. Once we made the decision to keep the agency I knew you'd do whatever it took to keep it running. Your job is here, and mine will be elsewhere."

I finally understood why Chad wouldn't talk about committing. He knew all along he'd be leaving and not returning. His future was set, while mine was falling apart. "We can still see each other, right? We can visit and speak on the phone?"

"I'm sure we'll talk, Rach, but let's be honest. As soon as I move, this thing between us will change. I never meant to fall for you. I thought it would be fun and help you get through your breakup."

"That's why you wanted me to go with Grayson. You thought we'd reconnect and you wouldn't have to worry about breaking things off with me."

He wouldn't respond.

"Chad, no. Don't do this to me. Not now. I've lost everything. I can't lose you too."

He frowned and turned his head away so I couldn't see his face. "I'll be around for a few months. It's not like I'm leaving tomorrow. We have time to be together."

I shook my head. "No. It's not fair. It won't work." "What do you mean?"

My heart was breaking all over again. I'd ruined things with Grayson, only to come home to discover there would be no future for Chad and I. "I think it's time to call a spade a spade. We've had some good times. You helped me, more than I'll ever be able to repay you, but I've lost too much. I can't handle falling harder for you and watching you walk out of my life. Right now I think I can manage if we're no longer a thing. It will hurt, but I'll learn to get by."

Chad took my hand and lifted it up to his lips. "I understand. I figured once you knew you'd call it quits. We were never meant to be, Rach. I'm just glad I got to know you. For what it's worth, I meant what I said. I do love you, but you and I both know it's not enough."

"It never is."

He stood to exit my apartment. I followed behind him. "So, I guess I'll see you at the office?" I needed us to remain friends. I couldn't bear losing him in my life completely.

He leaned forward and kissed me passionately on the lips. "You know, I don't have to go tonight. Tomorrow is a new day. Tell me you want me to stay, Rach. Say you want to have one final night together."

I faked a smile, determined not to lose my shit as I explained what I wanted from Chad. "I wish it were that easy. I wish I could ask you stay, because I want to feel what it was like to be in your arms one more time, but we both know what will happen. We'll go right back to the way it was, then finally get punched in the face with the truth when you have to leave. I've lost enough tonight. I can't handle being close to you while knowing it's a temporary fix. Truth be told, I think we both knew all along this wouldn't work. You came into my life when I needed you the most. I'm glad I know you, Chad. I hope we can remain friends, even if it's long distance. You're a sweet man. You made me feel alive in the midst of tragedy." I was getting choked up. "It's best if we end this for good, right here and now. I need to stop hurting long enough to heal. If this weekend has taught me anything it's that I haven't been focused on what was important to me."

"Your family you mean? It's always been about them, hasn't it?"

I nodded. "I suppose it has, not that it matters now. My marriage is over. Grayson doesn't need me anymore. I'm on my own, and it's time I learn how to manage it."

Chad kissed me again, this time keeping his lips on mine for a few seconds. "I'll see you in the office on Monday. We'll do lunch and go over what I need done while I'm on my trip."

Pretending to smile would have taken too much energy. I closed the door as he walked outside and sunk down to the floor beneath me.

I finally understood what rock bottom felt like.

Nothing could feel worse than what I was experiencing now. I was at a loss for words, with no motivation to get up and get over it. I'd lost too much to care what happened to me. I just wanted to die.

Chapter 34

Six months have gone by fast. I'd been in low places, and found that with time I could overcome my fears and forgive myself for the wrong choices I'd made in my life. I didn't have regrets, not any I'd want to change. I wasn't exactly in a happy place, but I was beginning to see the light at the end of the tunnel.

For a long while nothing felt right. I was lost, tortured by my own emotions on a daily basis. Things got worse once Chad relocated his side of the company to the West Coast. I think I cried for weeks, not because he was gone, we hadn't been involved since the night we called it quits. I was just lonely. I felt like my friend was gone. Even though I could still chat with him, it wasn't the same as having a lunch companion, someone who understood everything I'd been through.

Since Charles had been retired, the office was quiet. Things were going smoothly.

Stephanie visited me every other weekend, kind of like visitation when kids are young. Grayson and I had kept in touch. Truth be told, I missed our life, especially now that Chad wasn't around to distract me. It was like I needed time alone to see what I wanted. Anyway, when we spoke it was just about normal things. A few times we'd both break down. Up until last week we hadn't seen each other. Then, out of nowhere he asked me out on a date.

I was shocked.

Time had passed, giving me proof he wasn't involved with Kyla. Stephanie had been snooping around and found out her ex-friend was seeing someone new, having long forgotten about her tryst with Grayson.

So much for love.

As for me, well I took Grayson up on the offer. We'd planned to meet up on Friday night in Annapolis for some waterfront dining. We'd gone there for one of our anniversary dinners, so we knew how much we loved the cuisine.

I was pretty excited about seeing him. I wondered if he'd let himself go, or if he was still the stunning man who made me weak in the knees. According to our daughter, he'd been doing better. After some time seeing a therapist, he'd come to terms with what couldn't be changed. In all honesty, I think his affair was more trying on him than mine.

I was in a good place; one where I was open-minded, and ready to forgive. It had taken me a while. I'd lost a lot.

That Friday morning I woke up at the crack of dawn. I went into the office and got everything done early so I was able to have a half-day. Nothing was going to keep me from seeing Grayson and starting over as if we'd just met. My mind was made up. No matter how long it would take us, I knew he was the man I was supposed to be with. This was no longer about which man gave me the greatest pleasure. I wasn't blinded by lust. This was about something deep inside, a powerful love that could stand the test of time. I knew that now.

Stephanie called me three times during the afternoon. She was overjoyed about the two of us reconnecting, and according to her, so was Grayson. With nothing standing in our way, I hurried to prepare for a our special date, wearing something sexy, and adding a perfume he'd gotten me last Christmas. I spent too long on my hair, and messed up my makeup once before finally getting it right. Every detail had to be perfect. This second chance was all we were going to have. If we screwed this up now there was no going back. I had to live with that.

I don't even remember the forty minute drive to Annapolis, or the horrible traffic I had to endure to get there. I managed to find a close parking spot and hurried into the restaurant, hopeful he was there waiting for me.

After letting the hostess know about our reservations, she took me to our table and handed me a menu while I waited.

Five minutes passed.

Then ten.

Nearly twenty.

I tried calling his phone but got no answer. Figuring he was stuck in rush hour traffic, I ordered a glass of wine and tried not to worry.

Before I knew it, an hour had gone by and no Grayson.

While I tried his number again, I paid for my wine, figuring he'd changed his mind about us. Maybe Grayson wasn't as ready to move forward as me. Maybe it was too late for reconciling.

I made it to my car before Stephanie called. I ignored the first one, because I couldn't bear to break her heart with the news. Then she continued calling me until I finally picked up. "Honey, he didn't show."

"Mom," she sounded frantic. "It's Daddy. The neighbors found him out front unconscious. I'm trying to get to the hospital now."

"What? No. He's meeting me for dinner." I was in denial.

"Mom, you need to come. I don't know much. Mrs. Constance said she thinks it's his heart."

"His heart? Your dad is healthy as an ox. I'm sure he's going to be fine," I lied. I didn't want her driving while breaking down, especially in the city. "Where are they taking him?" I was already getting in my car prepared to speed to get to them.

"Hopkins. They're taking him to Hopkins. That's why I know it's bad. Why would they take him there if it wasn't?"

She had a point. "I'm on my way, sweetie. Please be careful. I'll see you in thirty minutes."

My drive into Baltimore was full of emotions. I kept thinking about the worst of scenarios, arriving and him already being gone. I wondered how long he'd been suffering, and if he'd been in a lot of pain, but tried to push through it to make our date. I wondered if this was a direct result of the toll our breakup had put on him.

My heart was shattering again, and I wasn't sure I was going to be able to handle any more bad news.

The parking garage was full when I arrived at the hospital. I managed to squeeze into a small spot and wedge my body between the opposing vehicle to exit. The elevator took forever to retrieve me, and just as I was about to make a beeline for the stairs, I heard the ding.

I dashed through the double doors of the emergency department, my nerves on high alert. Dizziness swept over me. I was freaking out, nervous and determined to get to Grayson. He had to know I loved him. I couldn't let something happen to him without him knowing that.

While the receptionist looked up his last name, I tapped my feet, searching the room for an open door I could run through to find him myself. Then she handed me a visitor's log I had to fill out. I'm not even sure if I wrote a name. I scribbled something and shoved it back toward her, taking the badge and darting for the double doors where I knew I'd find him.

There again, I stood waiting for someone to help me.

Finally the doors opened. I showed my badge and walked as I spoke to the nurse. "My husband. He was brought in earlier by ambulance. My daughter said it might be his heart." Just speaking the words out loud sent bile rushing to my throat. I'd done this to him. I'd sent him to his breaking point. His heart wasn't just broken over our breakup, it was shutting down. Tears filled my eyes once again as the relevance sunk in. I needed to see him; to know he was going to make it. A million scenarios were running through my mind, yet without answers I couldn't think of anything positive.

She brought me to a private room where I found Stephanie leaned over the bed, she backed away with tears in her eyes the moment she spotted me in the doorway. "Mom." She rushed toward me, throwing her arms around my neck. "I'm so glad you're here."

My eyes diverted to Grayson, who seemed to be awake, but groggy. "Hi," he barely managed to say. "I'm sorry."

I was at his side within seconds, taking his hand and gripping it. "Hi yourself. What happened?"

"He had a heart attack, Mom. The doctor just came in to talk to me. They said he had to get a stent put in. He just came back to the room about five minutes ago."

I kept my eyes on Grayson. "How are you feeling?"

He was crying. "I thought I was going to die alone."

I couldn't keep the tears from falling down my face. "You're too young to die on us. We still have a long life to live."

I ran my hands over his thick hair, appreciating he didn't try to turn away. "I had pressure last night, but thought it was something I ate." He was struggling to talk. A nurse came in the room to administer drugs into his IV.

"I hear you had quite a scare today. Don't worry, you're in great hands."

I waited until she finished to address Grayson again. "You should have called me. I would have taken you to the hospital."

"I didn't want to miss our date, Rachel."

This tore me to pieces. It didn't matter how much pain he was in. He wanted to see me; to start over, and nothing was going to keep him from it.

I raised his hand to my lips and kissed it. "You're so stubborn. You could have died."

"At least I'd die trying, babe."

"Are you two okay for a minute? I just need to make a call to my work."

Stephanie came up next to me to make sure we were listening.

"Sure. I've got him. Go ahead. We'll be here when you return."

Once she left the room I leaned forward and placed my lips on the side of Grayson's head. "I'm here for our date. Sorry I was late."

He managed to smile, even with an oxygen line sticking in his nostrils. "You look beautiful."

I couldn't say the same. I'd never seen him look so drained. "Try to stay calm. You need your rest."

"Please don't leave, Rachel. Don't go yet."

I squeezed his hand. "I'm not leaving. I'm staying right here until you can go home, and then I'll be there with you. I'm not letting you out of my sight until I know you're going to be okay."

"You don't have to stay with me. I know I'm not your responsibility."

It wasn't even an option for me. Being with Grayson was where I belonged. We'd no longer have an awkward transition. I had a reason to be close to him, to nurse him back to health. We could take it slow, and when the time came, we could have that second chance at happiness. "The next time I leave your side, it will be to move out of my apartment. I think it's time I come home. It's where I need to be." Then I added. "It's the only place I want to be."

We were both a mess. "I love you, Rachel."

"I love you too, Grayson. This time we'll get it right. I promise."

While he dozed off to sleep, I silently wept in the chair next to him. I'd almost lost him. Maybe God had intervened. I'd always believed everything happens for a reason. Whatever helped us find our way back to each other I was grateful. I vowed to never take our marriage from granted again. This time we'd do it right. We'd take care of each other. We'd communicate. We'd go to therapy. As long as I had him by my side, I knew we could make it.

It took me a while to get over the past, but once I did, there was no looking back.

Epilogue

I was sitting up in bed nervous about a meeting I'd have to attend with Chad. It had been close to a year since we were in the same room, and longer for when we called off our relationship. Sure, I'd had several video chats during monthly meetings, but other people were included. This however, would be completely different. At some point we'd be alone. I wasn't a fool. I knew I'd feel something, even though Grayson and I had been happily back together for months. I was content and satisfied. This wasn't the problem for me. The biggest hurdle was knowing Chad left with unresolved feelings. I suppose when we ended things so abruptly, I threw myself into my job and new lifestyle. I mourned the loss of him, and now he'd be close enough to touch.

I always told Grayson I'd never cheat; that if the roles were reversed I wouldn't have acted on impulse. Now, with the time spent trying to forget, I was afraid I couldn't control myself.

What if he wanted to hug me? Would I be able to let go?

We still chatted every once in a while, whether it be on the phone or email. He'd always be friendly, but never really mentioning what we shared together. Even though I was where I knew I belonged, I missed him. I missed his spunky sense of humor, and how he knew when I needed extra attention to get me out of a sour mood.

Grayson stirred and lifted his head, noticing me sitting up next to him. "Hey, babe. You doing alright?"

My worries weren't a secret. I'd discussed my feelings with Grayson, because in all honesty, if I did something irrational, I needed him to be prepared. "Maybe I shouldn't go to the office tomorrow. I'm sure they can video me in."

He rubbed his face and leaned on my leg. "Rachel, you're going to be fine. It's natural to feel nervous."

I faced him, determined to make a serious point. "Grayson, I'm scared. You know he was there for me when things were terrible between us. I'm grateful for his friendship."

"You're worried you might do something aren't you?"

I felt a knot in the pit of my stomach just bringing it up. Grayson had recovered from his heart attack, but not a day had gone by where I wasn't worried about his health. I knew I couldn't live without him, not comfortably. Since getting back together our relationship was stronger than ever. That's why I couldn't understand why one visit was making me question my sanity. "I know I don't love him, Grayson. You have to believe me. It wasn't anything like we have."

"I get it. It still hurts, but I get it. So, do you feel like you want to be with him?"

I knew his question was torture, albeit wasn't as hard as my answer would be. "I'm afraid I won't be in control of my own actions. Does that even make sense?"

"Yeah. I've got to be honest though, it doesn't make me feel comfortable either. Rachel, I know you. You're a good person, and sometimes because of that, you make decisions to appease others. This time you need to rethink the way you handle tough scenarios. If you have unresolved feelings there's nothing I can do. It hurts, but it's just another hurdle we'll cross together, as a couple. We can get through anything as long as we're open, remember what the therapist said?"

He was right. Our marriage counselor had explained this was necessary. No matter how hard the topic, it needed to be addressed.

I kissed the top of my husband's head. "I need to do this. I need to face him and let go of whatever unresolved feelings I have. Just know, I'll come home to you Grayson. I always will. I know you're worried, but please don't fret. Don't think the worst while I'm gone. It's one meeting. It's not like I'm going out of town. I'll be home for dinner, and I'll tell you all about how awkward the day was."

"I trust you, babe. I'm worried, but I know you'll make the right decision."

I cuddled my body up against his, feeling the need to provide comfort to his precious heart. "I love you."

"And I love you. It's always been you, Rachel."

It made me smile. I leaned up and kissed his lips. One chaste expression turned into a longer embrace. Before

I knew what was happening he'd adjusted us to where I was on top of him in bed. Our tongues mingled together, while my nightgown was being lifted over my head. Grayson move his ass to let me know he wasn't ready to go back to bed, not yet at least. I ran my hands up his bare chest, stopping when one of my palms was over his heart. I could feel it beating, reminding me how close I'd come to losing him before.

I leaned down and kissed him again, scooting off my husband so he was able to remove his boxer shorts. He shoved them down, rolling on top of me immediately. His hands began caressing my sensitive skin, while he kissed his way around my neck and then down to one of my breasts. His tongue traced a nipple in a circular pattern, his hand coming up and pinching the other. My body arched as his lips found mine again.

My legs came up and wrapped around his bare ass. He began setting a course for motion overtop of me, teasing me with his rock hard shaft. My legs were spread, ready to accept all of him like I'd done so many times before. It had taken us a while to be able to be intimate again, but once it happened I remembered he belonged to me. Nothing a little tramp could have done would change the fact that I'd always held his heart. I wasn't going to let six months ruin a lifetime of love we would share together.

Grayson breathed heavily against my ear. I knew he was about to enter me, to fill me with everything he had to offer. I tightened my grip around his back and prepared to be swept away with ecstasy.

Right as I was about to feel it, he lowered his body, kissing his way down my abdomen and then to my sweet spot below. I felt his mouth there, first tickling my clit, but then devouring my pussy. I gasped and let out a tiny cry as he lapped his way inside my opening, groaning when his tongue made contact with my juices. Grayson did a trick with his tongue, applying pressure to my clit he knew got me off. I dug my fingers into his hair, holding on while falling prisoner to his hot tantric persuasion.

While my body bucked, trying to recuperate, my husband came up and pressed his lips against mine. I could taste my release as our tongues meshed together.

Then, all of a sudden, I felt pressure below. He was sliding inside of me, giving me no time to catch my breath. I raised my hands above my head and let him take control, gliding his body over mine so practiced, like we'd done a million times before. He was slow, taking his time, because we had forever. His kisses were seductive, his movements graceful, as if he was handling precious cargo. I closed my eyes as chills ran from my lips to my toes, tingling in parts of me only lovers got to see.

He rolled us over, sitting me up so my body was straddling his. We held hands as I began my pace, riding him in a slow trot. I arched my back, feeling both his hands coming up and massaging my tender sensitive breasts. I reached between my legs, stroking my clit as my movements became more rapid. The easy pace was changing into a faster canter. I could feel my next orgasm coming to the surface. I tightened my ass and rocked over his as fast as possible, screaming out as pleasure overwhelmed me. At the same time, he grabbed my hips and kept me from moving. I watched his face scrunch up as he lost himself in euphoria.

Afterwards we remained connected. I rested my head on his chest while he brought his arms up and held me. "I know you'll come home to me, Rachel."

He was right. I would. I just hoped it was because I was able to handle myself properly, instead of getting lost in passion with another man for the second time in my life. "I promise I will."

I'd been at the office for fifteen minutes before I heard his familiar voice. My stomach was in knots, and I swore I'd looked at myself in the mirror six times while on the train. This wasn't like me to be so worried about self-control. I'd prided myself in being in control of every situation, yet here I was struggling to comprehend how one man could make me feel so unsure.

I watched the second hand on the clock move, slowly making it's way to the time I needed to report to the conference room. I'd received a memo on my email regarding the meeting. There would be two. The first would include upper management. The second would be a closed meeting to both CEO's – me and Chad.

My hands were shaking, and I half expected him to come in and say hello before we got started.

Finally it was time for the big reveal. I adjusted my skirt, remembering the way Grayson looked at me with worry when he saw what I'd chose to wear. I tried to reassure him, but there was no getting around the elephant in the room.

Once I entered, I took a seat furthest from where I

thought he'd sit. I pulled out my cell phone and played around, searching for recipes or anything to keep my mind off of Chad.

Then I heard his voice, getting closer, and finally out of the corner of my eyes noticed he'd sat right next to me. He was approaching my face. I prepared for his welcome, not really sure what to expect. "You look great, Rach," he whispered in my ear. I still hadn't had the nerve to glance in his direction. I was too afraid. I couldn't handle the way I knew he'd be staring at me. I wasn't able to see his hazel eyes gazing into mine. It would make me lose my self-control.

I clenched my knees under the table, waiting for someone to start talking about work, instead of it being brutally quiet.

A few minutes later the meeting began. I was able to breathe easier with the subject on both companies instead of Chad. He'd hired an assistant for the marketing side of the company. Officially, it was our annual meeting. We went over numbers for both entities, breaking down gains and losses. We talked about revenues and goals for the upcoming quarter.

When it was my turn, I did the same, keeping my focus on my spreadsheets instead of my neighbor.

An hour later the room cleared out, leaving me and Chad alone again. Before I could speak, he slid a folder in my direction. "I won't keep you long, Rach. There's just a few legal documents we need to take care of."

"Legal documents? You didn't ask the attorney to be present?"

"I had them draw everything up last week. Before you argue with me, why don't you take a look at my proposal?"

I glanced down at the paperwork, allowing my eyes to adjust for a second time when I couldn't believe what I was seeing. "This can't be right."

The legal document in front of me was stating the company was being transferred to my name. I would be the sole owner and CEO of Leviathan Agency, while Chad would have one-hundred percent ownership of the marketing company. "It's right, Rach. You've busted your ass on a company I wanted nothing to do with. It's your baby, and you deserve it."

I slid the papers back in his direction. "I can't accept this, Chad. It's very generous, but uncalled for. I'm perfectly happy with my position."

"Fine," he began tucking the papers away. "I'll sell it to someone else then."

"What?" I quickly pulled the documents back in front of me. "No. I don't want you to sell it."

"After speaking with my grandfather, we've decided it would be best. He wants you to have it, Rach, and so do I. You know he cares about you. According to the revised will, you were getting it regardless." He tapped on the paperwork. "Sign the papers and make it official. I know you don't want to be in here with me."

I still hadn't looked in his direction yet. "I never said that."

"You don't have to. I know you. Our situation may have changed, but a man doesn't forget a woman as special as you are."

"Stop." I covered my face and prayed I could keep my composure.

"Sorry if I overstepped. Just sign the damn papers and I'll get out of your hair."

Suddenly I realized we had little time to spend together and I was acting like an immature kid. I turned and finally let my eyes coast over that body I knew so well. "You really want me to have the company?"

"It's been yours all along. I'm just finally getting around to making it official. Sign the papers. Take control of the company. Make it your own. Change the name if you want."

"No. I wouldn't. Leviathan is a huge part of my life."

He kept staring at me, then nodded. "I know what you mean."

For a few seconds I felt like he was looking into my soul. My hands were shaking, and my palms were sweaty. I was uncomfortable, but didn't want to move an inch away from him. "I'm happy, Chad. I want you to know that." "I can tell. It's obvious. You look stunning."

I managed to smile, feeling the heat rush to my cheeks.

"How's Grayson?"

"He's doing well, thanks for asking."

"Is he treating you right, because you know, you always have another option. As far as I'm concerned, there's never going to be another like you."

"Don't say stuff like that," I whispered. "I'm committed to my marriage."

"I know you are." He reached over and brushed my cheek with the back of his hand. I closed my eyes and attempted to keep from reacting. "Walking away from you was the hardest thing I've ever done in my life. I regret it, but I know it was for the right reasons. I was never the man you needed, Rach. Your heart already belonged to someone else."

I wanted to argue with him, but what good would it do? He was right. I was with the man I loved. Chad represented a time in my life where I was at my lowest. He saved me, and for that I owed him a lifetime of respect and appreciation. "Thank you."

He kept his fingers on my chin. "Don't mention it. Just know, if that man ever treats you wrong, I'll be in California, with plenty of room to share."

I snickered. "We did have fun, didn't we?"

"It hasn't been the same."

I looked down at the papers and signed them. "I'll never be able to repay you for this."

"Look at it this way. If I ever need furniture, you can write it off on your account."

We both laughed. "Is there anything else you need from me?"

His brows furrowed. "No. If the attorney requests something I'll let you know. It's not really a huge change. People won't even notice. The marketing firm hasn't been here in a year. If you ask me, your employees will be thrilled. They never liked me."

"Yeah, I remember when I felt that way too."

He brought his face closer, almost to where he was touching me. "And how do you feel about me now?"

I couldn't close my eyes. We weren't touching, but it felt like we were. I licked my lips and replied. "I think you're the only man on the planet to make me feel like I could break my marriage vows. It makes me uncomfortable, because I know how easy it would be to fall into your arms again, but I know what that kind of pain feels like, and I refused to put myself and my husband through it again." I slid my chair back. "Thank you again for the company. I'll be paying Charles a visit very soon." I reached out my hand to shake his. "I guess this is it then?"

Chad stood, displaying his height. He glared into my eyes, as if pleading with me to reconsider. He leaned forward and let his lips linger on my cheek, then toward my ear. "I will always love you, Rach. Never forget it."

I watched him leave the room, then collapsed back down into the chair. By the time I managed to calm down, Chad had left the building.

I didn't stick around to make an official announcement. I needed to get out of there. While riding on the train, I focused on Grayson and how I'd kept control over my actions. A part of me wondered what would have happened if I gave in, but I knew I would have regretted it.

When I pulled up out front I saw Grayson mowing the lawn. He'd only been working three days a week after his heart attack, and relieved stress by doing light yard work from time to time. He stopped the riding mower and climbed off to greet me. "Hey, babe. Is everything okay? Did it go alright?"

"It's better than okay. You can retire. We're now the official owners of the Leviathan Agency. Charles and Chad gave me the company."

He hugged me and then pulled away. "Holy shit. That's amazing news. You've worked your ass off for it. Wow."

"It's all mine. I can't believe it."

"How did everything else go?" Of course he'd ask immediately.

"I won't have any reason to see or talk to Chad anymore, and I'm completely okay with it. I have a life here, and he's in California. I told you nothing would tear us apart again, Grayson, and I meant it."

We stood in the front yard hugging. I wanted to cry, not because I was sad, but more because I had closure. I could live the rest of my life without regrets. We'd be okay, and so would Chad.

The End

www.ingramcontent.com/pod-product-compliance
Lightning Source LLC
Chambersburg PA
CBHW051424170626
46809CB00006B/2307